# Sea To Shore Short Stories

# By The Children Of
# Combe Martin Primary School

Compiled by Stephanie M Turner

# Sea To Shore Short Stories

Compiled by Stephanie M Turner

Sasmjadahoha Publishing

ISBN 978-0-9929881-3-5


Sasmjadahoha Publishing
Email: books@sasmjadahohapublishing.com
Tel: (+44) 7546856165
www.sasmjadahohapublishing.com

A Note To The Reader

As an author, what I find most rewarding, is imparting my knowledge of 'The Story' to young aspiring writers. Then, to encourage these new authors to take the bud of an idea and develop it into a full flowering story of their own. Within these pages you will find an amazing collection of these stories. A collection full of imagination and wonder, the ordinary and the extraordinary, joy and sadness, from the depths of the ocean to the beauty of the moors.

Stephanie M Turner

# CONTENTS

ACKNOWLEDGMENTS


The children of Combe Martin Primary School, for their outstanding writing
and wonderful imaginations.

# The Blue Moon

The moon glowed brightly, big and full. But instead of wonderfully white, it was brilliant blue. This was very strange as a blue moon is as rare as pink cheese. Down below, even stranger things were happening. The Camel's Eye, the great rocky aspect of Combe Martin was beginning to move. Thud, thud, thud. Small white horses bucked against its stone legs as it stretched them across the water, something it hadn't done in so long. Leisurely, it circled its way around the rocks and away from the bay.

Time passed, and the camel was comfortably settled back on its shelf of rocks as ant sized figures crawled along its bumpy back. One of those was ten-year-old Noah. He was hiking up the rocky camel's head. When he reached the top he looked down the path to see how he would get back. He felt dizzy as he saw how far he would have to climb, so he settled down for a nap.

When Noah woke up, the sky above was dark and the snaky tide slithered up the rocks to where he was, the cloud rolling in over him. Once more the blue light of the moon glowed brilliantly and his ears caught the sound of thud, thud, thud. Stone by stone, rock by boulder, the camel strolled over the dark mirror of sea, crashing as it went. And still in the village, everyone slept.

The camel made its way to Ilfracombe, its head swaying slowly from side to side, Noah still sitting on its rocky back. They passed through Ilfracombe towards Woolacombe, where the camel stopped for a drink of fresh water from the large stone fountain, a feature of Woolacombe. It then splashed through the river Taw to Barnstaple and across Whitefield Hill.

As it climbed the steep hill, lights like aliens glowed ahead. They were from a car. Noah felt very scared. What if the people in the car saw him? What would he do? The car slowed to a stop and a young man got out. Noah knew him. He was Tommy Williams, the photographer. If he took a photo what would happen? Tommy lifted his camera and a white, blinding flash bounced off Noah's eyes. Tommy got back in his car and drove away, driving straight through the camel.

The camel continued its journey. Noah still on its back, felt very confused at what had happened. When they reached Combe Martin, the camel folded its legs underneath it and settled back in its place. Noah climbed down.

"Goodbye!"

He shouted to the rocky statue and made his way home.

When he got home his mother scolded him for being so late. But Noah couldn't focus on that. He was too busy wondering what had happened when the car drove through the camel, and what the photo would be like. Would he be in the photo? He went to bed thinking about that.

In the morning, Noah's mother sent him over the road to the shop to buy the Sunday paper. He handed the man the money and glanced at the front page. There was a photo, a picture of a blue moon shining over Whitefield Hill. The photographer couldn't see the camel.

As Noah grew, he thought a lot about his ride on the camel's back. Sometimes he was a little sad, that he would probably never get the chance to have that camel ride again. But when he slept, dreams of the rocky camel raced through his head.

As the camel waited for another hundred years to go for a walk, its stone heart felt a warm glow. For the first time in its history it had shared its journey with another living being. And whenever Noah stood on the camel's head, he felt a warm sensation below.

Jaycee Lorrimore

# X Marks The Spot

Many, many years ago a ship was sailing across the ocean. It was a stormy day and the water was rough. The crew, all pirates, tried their best to keep the ship afloat, but the howling wind lifted the boat and turned it over in the churning sea.

"We're going to die!"
Hollered the pirates as the ship sank to the bottom.

Five hundred years later, a young thirteen-year-old girl called Jay, was strolling along the shore of Combe Martin's beach. She was happily listening to her music and not taking much notice of anything around her. Suddenly she was startled when the blue sea shot up into the air.

"What?"
Yelled Jay as water splashed all over her making it hard for her to see.

Jay blinked and rubbed the sea from her eyes, then blinked again. In front of her was a very old ship.

"Arrgh me thinks we be 'avin' an adventure."
A voice came from somewhere. Jay spun around and saw pirates on the deck of the ship. She couldn't believe what she was seeing.

"Ye be comin' with us?"
The voice asked, and Jay realised it was one of the pirates. Thinking she was asleep on the beach and having a weird dream, Jay decided to go along with the pirate.

"Ok, I'll come."
She called out and began to swim towards the ship.

The pirates leaned over and pulled Jay onto the ship.

"Me thinks we be goin' to find treasure."

Said the captain.

"Me thinks ye got the map."

He said to Jay, pointing to her pocket. Jay put her hand in her pocket and was surprised when she pulled out a very old map.

"Take the wheel and lead us to the treasure."

So, with Jay steering the ship and following the very old map, they set sail. The map took them around an under-water village, Jay thinking she must definitely be dreaming, as she didn't get even a tiny bit wet. It took them over the giant killer whale, the whale didn't notice, and finally sailed up to Sandy Island.

The pirates climbed from the ship and followed Jay. The map led them under a waterfall and out of a rocky cave. Then, next to the twisted tree, where X marked the spot, they found the treasure.

"Ye found it. Me thinks you be a very good pirate Jay. We've got what we came lookin' for now we be off."

Jay blinked and found she was back on the beach in her village, Combe Martin. She was sure she had just woken from the strangest dream ever. She put her hands in her pockets and shrugged. Just as she felt a rough piece of paper, she heard a voice and a bubbling sound.

"Arrgh, Jay, you be a great pirate!"

Jay looked up and saw the pirate ship slowly sinking back into the sea, the pirates on board waving as they dipped beneath the waves. She pulled her hand out of her pocket and waved back. The piece of paper fluttered from her fingertips, and as it twisted and turned, Jay saw it was the map. Then it too sank into the ocean. It was then Jay realised she had really been on a pirate adventure and not asleep at all.

Joaquin Kane

# The Golden Girl

It was a beautiful day in Combe Martin. The sun shone brightly and the sand on the beach was warm and golden. Max and his sister Ruby were in the sea, waiting for some big waves to come rolling in.

Max glanced over his shoulder and saw a girl walk out of the water onto the beach. Her long blonde hair and tanned skin captured his attention, and Max thought about rocking the waves together in the moonlight.

"Hey Max!"
Yelled Ruby, snapping him out of his daydream. Max turned back just in time to see a huge wave coming towards them.

Max didn't have time to jump. The wave broke over his head and filled his mouth and nose with salt water. Max kicked his feet and flapped his hands, trying to fight his way back to the surface. As his head broke free and he took a gulp of fresh air, something grabbed his ankle.

Max was yanked back under the water. In the churning sea, he could just make out a long green tentacle wrapped tightly around his foot. It was pulling him down. Max struggled but he couldn't break away, the sea monster was too strong.

The surface of the sea began to disappear, and the light began to fade, as Max was pulled further down. He couldn't breathe and he was very scared. As his eyes slowly closed, Max saw a flash of gold. Then he was flying upwards and out of the water. Warm sunlight and fresh air greeted him and he breathed deeply. He felt arms about his waist and blinked the sea water from his eyes. It was the beautiful blonde girl he had seen on the beach.

The girl smiled and swam to the shore, still holding onto Max. Ruby was running up and down the edge of the water screaming for her brother. She stopped when she saw the girl help Max to his feet and out of the sea.

"Max, Max, are you ok?"
Ruby squealed, throwing her arms around him. Max nodded and turned to the girl.

"Thank you. Thank you so much, you saved me."
Ruby let him go and threw her arms around the girl.

"You saved him, he was drowning, but you saved him. You must come home and let our parents thank you too."
The girl smiled again, a beautiful gleaming smile. Her blonde hair shimmered in the sunlight and her skin glowed.

"I'm glad I saved your brother but I can't come home with you. I have to go back to my own home."
Ruby was about to argue but Max stopped her. He took Ruby's hand and tugged her to his side. There was something about the girl, something about the way she looked, she was too perfect.

"It's ok Ruby. She has to go."
He said to his sister and nodded towards the girl. The girl gave him her beautiful smile and walked away, towards the water. Max and Ruby watched as she dived under a breaking wave. But they didn't see her come up, and they never saw her on the beach again.

Katrina Phillips

# Prince Of The Palace

It was the school holidays and Red, Mike and Jake had nothing to do. They were sitting in Red's garden when he had an idea.

"Want to go swimming?"
Suggested Red.

"Definitely."
The other two replied together.

"Ok, go and get your swimming gear and meet me back here."
Red told them.

The boys didn't take long to get changed, and quickly they were happily strolling down to the Combe Martin beach. Jake was the first one in the water. He waded out and stopped.

"Hey it's warm over here."
He called to the other two. Red and Mike joined him. Jake was right, the water was very warm just in that spot.

"But how?"
Mike wondered aloud to the others.

"Let's look underwater."
Suggested Red.

They put on their goggles and dived under the water. Below, on the seabed they could see a small light buried in the sand. Red, curious, swam down and grabbed it. The moment he touched it there was a flash of light, so bright the boys shut their eyes. When they opened them again they discovered they were not wearing their swimming shorts. Instead they were wearing T-shirts and shorts made of scales.

"What...?"

Red gasped. He didn't finish his sentence as he saw Mike and Jake staring at him in shock, he was talking underwater.

Mike and Jake tested their own voices and found they could talk underwater too.

"You do know this means we are breathing underwater as well."
Red told his friends.

"So if we can breathe and talk underwater we're not entirely human anymore." Mike added. "How cool is that?"
They were all very excited and swam about enjoying the experience.

At first they seemed to be alone. After a while, Jake noticed there were other people swimming near to them and they were all talking too, even the fish and sea creatures. In wonder, the boys swam closer, and to their astonishment found themselves in front of a huge underwater palace.

The door to the palace was enormous, reaching far above them and it was covered in glittering diamonds. Jake looked at his friends and could see the dare in their eyes. He took up the challenge, lifted his hand and knocked hard on the shining door. The door opened slowly. On land it would have creaked, but here under the sea it swished.

The boys hung in the water in suspense. It seemed to be taking a very long time for the door to open. Finally, a giant sized half shark, half human, guard wearing a tunic stuck its head through the gap.

"Who are you!"
He boomed in a deep voice.

The boys were terrified, but before any of them could answer, the half shark swept them inside the palace. Luckily for the boys, the guard wasn't very fast. As it slowly pushed the door closed, the three turned and swam away from it further into the palace.

They swiftly swam along deserted passageways, trying to find another way out. Red took the lead and pointed to a light up ahead. It was a passageway with walls covered in bright shining gems.

"Oh that's what's making the light."
Red called out over his shoulder.

"Help me!"
A voice came from one side of the passageway. The boys stopped swimming. They could see a small door in the wall, and through a crystal glass window saw a face peering out at them. He had human form.

The three boys could see a latch on the door and lifted it. They pushed the door open, it was heavy and took all of their effort. The young man swam out.

"Thank you so much. You have rescued me. I'm the prince of the palace. The guard imprisoned me here in this room and sent all of my people away from the palace. He told them I had left. For so long I have been trapped here. Come with me, I can lead you out of here."

Red, Mike and Jake followed the prince along more passageways until they came to a door similar to the front door, but not as big. It was a lot easier to open. They swam through it and came out into the walled palace garden. It was overgrown with seaweed. The prince led them through the garden gate and they could hear people.

Soon the three boys and the prince came upon the people who stopped and stared as they saw their prince. They surrounded him. The prince spoke to the people and explained what the guard had done. It made them angry. The people hammered on the diamond door until the guard opened it. They dragged the guard from the palace and threw him out of the kingdom.

The prince was very grateful to Red, Jake and Mike. He opened the palace doors and let everyone in. The kingdom celebrated the release of their prince and the prince rewarded the three boys.

"I will make you knights of my kingdom. You are welcome here anytime."
Instead of laying a sword across their shoulders, he touched them each with a shiny gem.

"Take the gems, and anytime you want to breathe underwater hold them in your hand."
After the celebrations, Red, Mike and Jake returned to the beach. But it was only the beginning of their underwater adventures.

Finley Sparks

# **Dawn**

Justin ran. His heart was beating fast as his feet pounded against the earth of the path. The tall trees of Ladies' Wood, on the edge of Combe Martin, surrounded him. Above him he could see the dark sky, in front of him just a glimmer of light.

Justin had to stop for breath. He leaned against the huge trunk of an old oak tree, trying to keep his panting quiet. The woods were silent, deserted, or so it seemed, but Justin knew he wasn't alone.

A crunch came from nearby, then a rustle. Justin held his breath, hoping he wouldn't be seen, or smelt. He huddled down in a crouch, peering around the trunk. Glowing yellow eyes, like flames, flickered amongst the bushes. Heavy deep breathing and low growling echoed around him. Justin trembled.

Thick, thundering footsteps slowly crept closer. Justin waited. First one large head, then another, began to take shape from out of the shadows and still he waited. As the breathing got closer and closer, Justin bolted from his hiding place.

He took off at speed, flying along the path, down towards the valley and the safety of the village. Behind him he heard the demons crashing through the bushes, chasing him, getting closer.

Justin leapt off the path and rolled down a rocky bank. He felt something fly over his head, heard a thud and an angry growl. He scrambled to his feet and took off again. In the distance he could see lights, street lights, the village, but he wasn't safe yet.

Taking in as much air as he could, Justin raced towards the lights. He glanced above and saw the first flash of dawn. Relief flooded through him. He would escape the beasts behind him. A spark of sunlight rose, just as Justin fled out of the darkness of the woods into the coming day. He heard shrill howls behind him, further away. Completely exhausted and out of breath, Justin finally stopped and slumped to the pavement. Far in the distance he heard more howls as the sky lightened. The dawn had saved him, the demon wolves were back hiding in the depths of Ladies' Woods.

William Smallridge

# School Outing

The bus was filling up as Daniel waited his turn to climb on. He carefully pulled himself inside and heard the doors slide closed behind him. Slowly he made his way to the back, hoping to get one of the single seats, but Shelley and Lola had already taken the first ones. Daniel scrambled across the seats to the very last set, but was pushed violently out of the way by Stan, who sat down with a proud grin on his face.

"Mine."

He said with satisfaction, stretching his legs across the seat so Daniel couldn't sit down. Daniel sighed and turned around looking for another seat. There was just one gap left, next to Connor, another boy who would tease him.

Daniel took the seat next to Connor and closed his eyes. He didn't want to be on the bus and he definitely didn't want to go on this school trip. He wanted to be at his old school, where the other kids knew him and liked him. None of these kids did, they didn't know anything about him. "Give it a try." His mum had said that morning, and he would, but it didn't seem to be working. A great first day this was turning out to be.

Connor elbowed him, making it clear he wanted more room, so rather than give Connor more excuses to have a go at him, Daniel moved right to the edge of the seat. He folded his arms across his chest and tried to make himself as small as possible.

The bus pulled away from the school. Daniel still had his eyes closed and the gentle motion soon made him doze off. A sudden jolt woke Daniel. They had reached their destination. Daniel tried to stand up but was shoved aside by Connor, knocking him to the floor. Connor laughed, treading on Daniel's fingers as he scrambled off the bus.

Daniel pulled himself up onto his knees.

"Get out of the way!"

Yelled Stan behind him, kneeing him in the shoulder and knocking his backpack from his back. The pack went flying and Stan crunched his foot down on it.

"Squashed lunch then."

Whispered Daniel to himself.

"Come on you lot, off the bus."

Called Mr Murphy the bus driver. Shelley and Lola slid past Daniel, giggling at him on the way. Daniel finally got to his feet and slumped towards the door. He was last.

Daniel stepped off the bus. Slowly and with great care he plodded to an empty bench and sat down. He felt cool salty air on his face and smiled. The bus had been hot and stuffy, but here by the sea the air was fresh. Daniel dipped his hand into his pack and pulled out his crushed lunch and a bottle of water. He drank most of the water, bit into a flattened sandwich and shrugged.

"Still tastes ok."

He murmured.

"What did you say?"

Connor asked, right into Daniel's ear, making him jump. Then Connor ran off before Daniel could answer.

A car pulled up alongside the bus and a woman with a dog climbed out. Daniel heard the panting of the dog and recognised the bright yellow jacket the dog was wearing.

"Lucy?"

Daniel laughed as the dog put her head in his hand and licked his palm.

"I got a call love, from your teacher. She said you were struggling without Lucy."

His mum explained in a hushed voice. Daniel grinned. He was a lot happier now Lucy was by his side.

Daniel's mum left him with his dog and drove off home. Connor, Stan, Shelley and Lola strolled over.

"How come you're allowed your dog on this trip?"

Asked Stan nastily. Daniel took a deep breath.

"She's my guide dog. I'm partially sighted."

He told them.

"Oh!"

Exclaimed Stan.

"That must be rough."

He added. Daniel shrugged.

"Used to it, and people treating me like I'm an idiot or something."

He said stroking Lucy's back.

"And it shouldn't give you an excuse to bully me."

He added.

Even with his partial blindness, Daniel could make out their red cheeks. All four dropped their heads, turned around and quickly walked away. Daniel grinned and hugged his dog. They would never be his friends, but he didn't think they would bully him again either. Suddenly the day had got a lot brighter.

Erin Cass

# The Old House

Tom sat in the lounge of his very old house. Opposite, a young reporter from a local newspaper, held a mug of tea in both hands as he listened intently. He was writing an article on old houses in and around the village of Combe Martin, and Tom's house fitted perfectly into that category.

"This old place is over two hundred years old."

Tom said, waving his hand around the room.

"How long have you owned it?"

Justin questioned.

"Just over a week now, but I've known the house all my life, and I know its history well."

Tom replied. Justin finished his tea and lifted his notebook in anticipation. This house, more than any of the other houses he had visited, had a feel of interest about it. He leaned forward a little in his chair and waited for Tom to begin.

"Like I said, I've known this house all my life. When I was a boy, I would come up here into the woods and play. There were rumours about this old house, and all of us kids used to try and get close, to look in the windows, but we were always too scared to do it."

Tom leaned back in his chair and gazed out of the big wide windows into the sprawling garden beyond. He had a little smile on his face. Justin waited patiently. Tom blinked and continued with his story.

"Apart from the rumours, the house never belonged to anyone for long. Years would go by and it would stay empty. Then someone would move to the village and buy it. But they never stayed more than a couple of months. They would move out and leave it empty, and it would be up for sale again. I hoped and hoped no one would buy the house and stay. I wanted it, to keep it as it was.”

Tom paused and once again looked out the window. The only sound was the slight noise of Justin's pen as he rapidly wrote down Tom's words.

“Why did you want it so much?” Justin asked, breaking the silence. Tom settled back in his chair and took a breath. Then with a tiny shrug he spoke.

“Over the years I found I wanted to know about the history of the house. So I went and asked about and learnt everything I could. The Martin family bought the land here in the woods and built the house. They owned it for a hundred years. Three generations kept the house, but the last ran out of money and had to let it go. A wealthy young woman called Catherine came to Combe Martin and fell in love with the house. She was engaged to be married and knew the house would be perfect for raising a family. Catherine moved in a week before her wedding. She wanted to make sure the house was ready for her and her husband.

Catherine was to be married on her twenty first birthday. Everything was planned to perfection, and she was so excited as the days ticked by. Her white lace wedding dress hung in her wardrobe, her wedding jewellery in a box on her dressing table.

Then disaster struck. On the eve of the wedding, Catherine had been out walking in the grounds. She had picked a bunch of wild flowers and returned to the house to put them in water. She took the flowers to her bedroom, and couldn't resist lifting her wedding dress from the wardrobe to look at it.

Instead of returning it to the wardrobe, Catherine hung it from the door, so she could look at it through the night. It was a chilly evening, so she lit the fire in her room to warm it before she went to bed.

With everything prepared for the wedding, Catherine settled in bed. Her family and friends were arriving in the morning, and she would meet her husband-to-be at the church. Catherine smiled to herself as she closed her eyes. The last thing she saw before she fell asleep was the white lace dress glowing in the firelight.

A crackling and popping woke Catherine. The room was too bright, but she couldn't see. Thick smoke was everywhere and it was hot. Flames spread across the floor from a log that had rolled from the fire. Catherine jumped from bed but the door was blocked by the fire. She yanked the window open, but as the air rushed in the flames got worse. Catherine was trapped. As the smoke and flames took her, her one thought was that she would never wear the white lace dress."

Justin had barely written any of what Tom told him. He was concentrating so much on Tom's words he had forgotten to write down the story. Tom seemed far away, his thoughts deep in the past. Justin realised Tom had stopped speaking and coughed.

"What happened then?"
He asked. Tom took a deep breath.

"Only Catherine's room got burnt. Some villagers saw the flames and rushed to help, but they were too late to save her, and strangely, the lace dress was hardly touched by the fire. When Catherine's fiancé found out she was dead, he went to her burnt out room and died of a broken heart.

It was then, after the fire, that no one stayed long in the house. Rumours went around that it was haunted, that Catherine and her fiancé would never rest until they found one another."

"Do you believe the rumours?"
Asked Justin. Tom smiled and shrugged. Justin felt the interview was over, so he took his notebook and said goodbye to Tom. Justin drove down to the village and stopped at a café. He would have a cup of coffee and write up his notes in more detail, he thought. Reading through his notes he realised something was missing.

"Excuse me. Could you tell me Tom's surname, the man who owns the Martin house in the woods?"
The café owner frowned.

"No one owns the old Martin house. It's been empty for years. There is a story, about a young woman called Catherine and her fiancé Tom, who both died in the house, but that happened about a hundred years ago."
Justin put down his notebook and picked up his coffee. He had the strange feeling that he had just interviewed a ghost.

Wayne De'Athe

# Black Sea

One night a huge storm thundered off the shore of Combe Martin. The enormous waves crashed over the deck of a ship, dragging it onto the rocks. The ship was stuck with a gaping hole in its side.

The storm passed and by morning the sea was again calm, the sun shining brightly. Aila jumped out of bed and looked out of her window. Her house was on the cliff and overlooked the beach. At first everything looked normal to her, then she noticed the sea looked a strange colour. Instead of its usual sparkling blue, it was black.

Aila ran downstairs, out of the house and down the path to the beach. She dashed along the walkway to her favourite place, the rock pools. All around her the water looked thick and gooey. The waves were slow and as they touched the rocks and sand, they left black blobs.

Aila was worried. She knelt down on the walkway and put her hand into a rock pool. She felt something sticking to her fingers. When she lifted her hand out, it was covered in the black stuff, but there was something else too, a little cluster of sea creatures.

Aila gently wiped away the black, and underneath found an edible crab, a shore crab, a cushion starfish and a blenny fish all piled together, glued by the black. Holding the animals carefully, she ran back to her house, she had an idea.

Back in her bedroom, Aila lowered the creatures into her fish tank. She swirled them about and they separated, the black coming off. Aila smiled to herself with relief, but she was very worried about the rest of the rock pools and the sea creatures.

Aila stared into her tank wondering what to do. The blenny swam to the top and stuck its head out.

"Thank you for helping us."

It squeaked. Aila couldn't believe it.

"You can talk."

She exclaimed in surprise. The blenny wiggled.

"Yes all of us can. It's just humans don't usually hear us. Our home, the sea, is in great danger. The storm last night broke a ship and it spilled black oil into the water. The oil will kill the animals and the plants, but you can help get rid of it."

"How?"

Asked Aila.

"You know the rock pools very well. We have seen you there many times. You have to go to the biggest, deepest one with your little net. Put it in the pool as deep as it will go. Then call for the Mother Pearl. She will come and tell you what to do. But you must hurry."

Aila grabbed her rock pooling gear and ran back down to the beach. More of the black oil was creeping onto the sand. Many of the other villagers were there. They had buckets and were trying to wash the oil from the sea birds. They were so busy they didn't notice Aila run past them down the walk way.

Aila found the rock pool and knelt down. She dipped her net in, sliding it down until the water reached her shoulder.

"Mother Pearl, Mother Pearl, can you hear me?"

Aila felt a tug on her net. She lifted it from the pool and inside saw a beautiful shimmering pearl.

"The sea needs you."

Aila spoke to the pearl. The pearl spoke back.

"Take me to where the ship is on the other side of the rocks."

Aila held the pearl in her hand and began to climb over the rocks. She had to climb high and then scramble down. Below her she could see the wrecked ship.

"What now?"

She asked the pearl.

"Put me in the water near the hole."

Mother Pearl told her. Aila did as she asked. At first nothing happened, then Aila heard a sucking sound. Her eyes widened as she saw the black, gooey oil begin to flow back into the hole. Soon, all of the oil was inside the ship. Aila jumped with joy. Mother Pearl floated on the now clear blue sea.

"Thank you Aila. I would have been trapped in the rock pool under the oil if you hadn't found the sea creatures and heard them. But because of you, I was able to clean the sea. Now the sea and animals are safe again."

Aila smiled. She felt so happy and proud that she had been able to help. She watched as Mother Pearl slowly sank beneath the waves, then jumped up and ran back to the beach. All of the oil had gone.

The villagers looked at the sea in wonder, but Aila didn't stop to explain. She didn't think anyone would believe her. She ran home and lifted the sea creatures from her tank and put them in her bucket. Carefully, she took them back to the rock pools and let them go. The blenny flicked its fins like it was waving, and then they all sank under the crystal clear water, safe once again in their home.


Ebony Hook

# Haunted Hole

Wilf sat in his lounge with his face in his hands.

"I'm bored."

He moaned.

"Then go to the beach."

Said his mother. Wilf thought for a moment. The beach was his favourite spot in Combe Martin, and it was a hot day. He jumped up and ran from the house. Faster and faster he ran, all the way down the village to the seaside. When he got there he was hot and very thirsty. The beach café was open so Wilf went in for a nice cold drink.

Wilf sat at a table near the window. He sipped his drink and looked out across the beach. The sand was golden and the sea sparkled, little diamonds of light bouncing along the gentle waves.

"Bet you don't know about the haunted part of beach."

Said Bill, the oldest fisherman in the village.

"What haunted part? There's no haunted part of beach."

Wilf replied. The old man laughed.

"I'll show you."

Wilf was curious, so he finished his drink and followed Bill out of the café. Bill led him down the walkway, across the sand and around the jagged rocks. There was no one about. Bill pointed to a gap in the cliffs.

"There. They go in but they don't come out."

He told Wilf in a hushed voice. Wilf still didn't believe him.

"Go and see for yourself."

Old Bill grinned with a shrug. Wilf, determined not to appear scared, strode across the rocks to the gap. He climbed up to the rough edge of the hole and peered inside. It was very dark. He pulled himself up and crawled just inside.

"Huh, nothing here as I thought."

He said out loud.

Wilf backed out of the gap. He was going to tell old Bill straight that there was nothing there. As he turned his head away from the hole, something grabbed his shirt. Wilf shrieked. A small furry creature was hanging onto his T-shirt by its teeth. Wilf scrambled down the rocks, the creature still attached to him. He heard a bellowing laugh behind him. Bill was standing nearby, holding his tummy. Tears were rolling down his old face as he laughed at Wilf.

"What is it?"

Wilf cried, holding his T-shirt out where the furry animal clung.

"I don't know."

Giggled Bill.

"You said it was haunted. Well this isn't a ghost."

Wilf replied furiously, giving the little creature a shake.

"But they do go in and don't come out again. Well except when someone like you goes in and one of them grabs a hold."

Bill told him still laughing.

"So what do I do with it? It won't let go."

Asked Wilf.

"You have to take it home and look after it, like a pet. It will let go then."

Bill explained. Wilf let out a big sigh. He didn't want the furry thing, didn't know what to feed it, or how to look after it."

"It will let you know."

Bill said, guessing what Wilf was thinking.

Wilf plodded back across the beach. He was cross with old Bill for tricking him and he really didn't want the furry creature. But he didn't know what else he could do but take it home. At least it might let go of his shirt then.

Once home, Wilf went up to his room. He didn't want to have to explain the creature to his mum. He shut his door and flopped onto his chair. As soon as he sat down, the animal let go.

"Please keep me safe. I'm nice and furry and cuddly. I don't eat much and I won't get in the way. It's lonely in that hole. Old Bill is right. When we go in we don't come out, unless one of us finds someone nice, like you."

Wilf sat in shock as the creature spoke. He looked at it. Its eyes were big and round and it was cute and cuddly. Wilf suddenly felt very friendly towards it, and he knew he would keep it as a pet, and he would keep it safe.

Callum Emery

# Cheetah Versus Octopus

Once upon a time in the village of Combe martin, there lived two boys, Cally and Kyran. They both loved animals, but would often quarrel over which animal was the best. Cally argued his favourite animal, the cheetah, was best because it was the fastest animal on earth. Kyran disagreed. He said the octopus, his favourite animal, was best because it was the strongest creature in the ocean and would save anyone who was drowning. One sunny day was the day he changed his mind.

Kyran and Cally were on the beach. It was hot and sunny and perfect for swimming. Cally didn't want to go in the water, but Kyran loved the sea and dived straight in. He swam and swam, further and further out. He was a good swimmer and often went far out.

After a long time, Kyran stopped and turned in a circle. There was nothing around him but water. He couldn't see any land. He couldn't see the shore. He shivered. He was lost and frightened. As he trod water he thought about his favourite animal, the octopus, it would save him, he was sure. Suddenly, he felt a tug on his leg. Then he was being pulled under the water. An enormous octopus, his favourite animal was pulling him down.

Kyran couldn't scream and he couldn't escape. He really had thought the octopus would save him, but it was trying to drown him. Kyran wriggled and struggled, but it was no good. Then someone was beside him, Cally, his best friend and Mr Alfie, the lifeguard. Together they pulled Kyran free of the octopus and dragged him to the surface. Mr Alfie pushed both the boys into his boat and took them back to the beach.

"Thank you, both of you."
Gasped Kyran. Cally smiled at his friend.

"So, the cheetah's best, yes?"
Kyran nodded and laughed. His friend was right. But as they sipped the drinks
Mr Alfie bought them, he did wonder what Cally would do if he was being
chased by one.


Noah Jewell

# Captain's Cats

It was late at night on Halloween. The sea was crashing hard against the rocks, higher and higher, throwing the fish out of the water onto the dark slippery walkway near the beach.

A ship appeared out of the murky waters into the bay of Combe Martin. There were jagged holes in the old wooden sides and its sails were torn. It was a wreck, a ghostly wreck. On board, the captain's cats, Skeleton and Sand, were as usual fighting.

"Stop!"
Shouted the captain.

"We are in Combe Martin. Maybe our crew, our friends are here."
He said to the cats, lowering his voice. The cats stopped fighting.

"Aye captain."
They both meowed together.

The captain lifted his cats from the deck and stared out across the bay. He could see children dressed in strange costumes and devilish masks, running around with pumpkin shaped buckets swinging from their hands. But he couldn't see any of his crew. He didn't know what the children were doing or why, and he didn't know what year it was.

As the children collected their sweets and treats for Halloween, the captain watched and waited, hoping his crew were amongst them. But they were not. Instead, out of the dark night appeared his enemy, the Dog pirates. Barking and howling, their hackles raised, the Dog pirates jumped into the sea and swam to the ghost ship.

The captain and his cats stood on deck and waited. The Dog pirates arrived, but there were no ladders or ropes for them to climb to board the ghost ship.

"You can't escape us!"

Barked the Dog pirate captain.

"Where's my crew?"

The captain hollered down to them.

"Give us your ship and we will give you your crew."

Yapped the Dog captain.

Skeleton and Sand meowed to each other, then whispered to the captain. He grinned and leaned over the side of the ship.

"Ok. You can board as long as you bring my crew with you. The ship will then be yours."

Dog captain nodded his shaggy head. Suddenly, the churning sea began to pop as the captain's crew appeared, one by one. The captain threw down the ropes and Dog captain and his pirates climbed, each one carrying a crew member on his back.

Once on deck Dog captain bared his teeth to the captain.

"Here are your crew. Now you all jump overboard and I take your ship."

The captain bent his head sadly.

"Aye, but first I have a gift for you."

Dog captain grinned triumphantly as the captain lifted his arms. Then Dog captain squealed in pain as Skeleton and Sand flew at him with their ghostly claws outstretched. Dog captain backed up trying to get them off, but they clung on with their sharp claws, scratching and biting him. He toppled overboard into the dark deep water. His pirates, too afraid to fight without their captain jumped over too.

The captain and his crew leaned over and watched them swim as fast as they could to the shore. As the captain laughed at the shaggy Dogs, he heard a sound just below, a fierce meowing. Skeleton and Sand were once again fighting, arguing over who had scared the Dogs away the most.

The captain grabbed each of his cats by the scruff of their necks and hauled them back on board.

"Stop!"

He shouted.

"Aye captain."

Said the cats together.

"We have our crew back. Let's set sail for a new adventure."

Skeleton and Sand glared at each other as the ghostly wrecked ship slowly sank beneath the waves of Combe Martin bay, unseen by the children running around the village collecting their Halloween treasures.

Skye Ovington

# Overflow

There were two young farmers who lived near Combe Martin. They worked hard on their farm, cutting fields, bailing and looking after the cattle. They just about made a living but it was a struggle.

One long day they dozed off in one of the fields. James woke up hearing a sound. It was a gurgling, bubbling noise. He shook Jack awake and they ran back to the farm. The slurry pit was about to overflow. James tried to turn the pump off but it wouldn't stop. Jack joined in and finally the pump gave up and fell to pieces. Luckily for them it stopped working before the slurry overflowed onto the farm.

"I've had enough!"
Shouted James.

"Everything is falling apart around here."
Jack didn't like to see his friend upset. He knew of a person who could help.

"Wait here James. I have to go and see someone."
Jack said and drove off in his tractor.

James waited for hours for Jack to return but his friend didn't come back that night. Miserably, James went to bed thinking Jack had left him to look after the run down farm by himself. He thought Jack had gone to work somewhere better.

In the morning, James got up and plodded out of the farmhouse. He wasn't looking forward to his day alone. But there was a surprise waiting for him. Jack was sitting in a brand new John Deere tractor.

"What, how?"
Exclaimed James. Jack grinned.

"Hop up. I've got loads to show you."

Jack drove the tractor around the farm buildings. He pointed. James peered out and saw a new modern slurry pit. Nearby was something James didn't understand.

"It's a biomass boiler and it will make us rich."
Explained Jack.

"What does it do.?"
Asked James.

"It turns the slurry into fuel and fertilizer. We won't get any more overflows and we can sell what we don't use."
James smiled. He didn't know how his friend had managed to get it all installed and working overnight, but he was very happy that he had.

With the farm working well, the two young farmers, James and Jack, did become rich. The years went by and the two friends grew old. But they now had sons of their own to pass their farm and its riches onto, leaving them to enjoy their old age peacefully.

Kurt Dennis

# New Family

Twin sisters, Roe and Rosella, had no parents or anyone else to care for them. They were nine years old, small, with shaggy brown hair. As long as they could remember they had lived in a tiny hut near the beach of Combe Martin, looking after each other. No one knew they were there, and no one knew they were alone.

The sisters caught fish and wild berries for their food, and sometimes found useful things washed up on the beach. But they only went searching at night. One night, as the moon rose silver bright in the dark ink blue sky, the girls went walking along the beach. No creature moved, and the only sound was the gentle wind blowing and the soft sea swaying back and forth.

"Ouch."
Grumbled Roe. Something sharp was poking out of the sand, digging into her foot. She pulled it from the ground and saw it was a beautiful purple and turquoise gem.

"Oh, it's lovely."
Exclaimed Rosella.

"It has something written on it."
Said Roe, holding it up to the moonlight.

"I give you…"
She read to her sister.

"What?"
Replied Rosella excitedly. Roe shrugged.

"That's all it says."

"Not much use to us then."
Rosella grumbled as she stomped off towards the cliffs. Roe ran after her.

"Rose, don't be miserable. Come on let's go in the caves. The sea might have washed up some good stuff."
Rosella smiled as her sister caught up. She couldn't stay angry with her for long.
The caves were dark, just a little light from the moon showing them the tunnels. The girls were used to this and were not afraid. They spent so much of their time in the caves they knew each turn by heart.
"Nothing!"
Moaned Rosella.
"Don't be sad. We always find something."
Roe chirped, trying to cheer her sister up.
"Not tonight Roe. I'm hungry and tired, let's go home, there's nothing here."
Rosella muttered.
"Sometimes I just wish we weren't so alone."
She added as she turned back towards the cave entrance.
A loud rumbling and cracking sound came from all around them. The girls clung to each other in fear. Then the cave floor opened and they fell, down, down they went until they felt water. The sea covered them and dragged them even further down. Still holding onto each other, Roe and Rosella were tugged and pulled into an underwater cave.
The cave glowed purple and turquoise, and on a rock they saw a group of mermaids.
"It's all right. You can breathe and speak."
One of the mermaids said in a sing-song voice.
"What's happened to us?"
Questioned Rosella.
"Look at the gem. What does it say?"
Rosella shrugged.
"Nothing."
She whispered miserably.
"Wait Rosella. Look!"
Squealed Roe, holding the gem out to her sister.
"I give you a family."
Rosella read with a frown.
"We can be your family. You will never be alone again. We will take care of you."

The mermaid explained with a smile. Roe took Rosella's hands and nodded. Rosella grinned back, her eyes widening as she watched her sister's hair change to long silky blonde.

"Your hair!"
Shrieked Roe.

"It's turned blonde."

"Mine? Yours has too. And, oh Roe, we have tails, look."
Roe looked down and both had tails covered in purple and turquoise scales.

"Now you are part of our family. You won't ever be alone again. Come and explore the sea."
The mermaid beckoned. Roe and Rosella joined the other mermaids and began their new life under the sea.

Milly Staddon

# Purple Heather

Max and his parents set off for a picnic on the moors. They hadn't been for a few weeks and Max was looking forward to it. As they drove, Max looked out of the window. The moors were different from their last visit. Now all Max could see was purple. Layer upon layer of beautiful purple heather.

They pulled up at their favourite picnic spot. Max's mum and dad got the table, rug and hamper from the boot and began to set it all up.

"Can I go for a walk?"
Max asked.

"Don't go too far then."
His mum replied.

Max set off along a path. The heather was all around and stretched as far as he could see. In the distance, Max could make out a tree standing by itself. He decided to make his way towards it. Max walked and walked for what seemed like hours, yet he never got closer to the tree. He stopped a moment to rest. He was hot, his face a bit sweaty. He wiped his eyes with his hands, and when he looked up, all he saw was an enormous brown trunk covered in giant green leaves.

Max was afraid. He didn't know where he was or where his parents were, and he didn't know how to get back. He turned in a circle and spotted a little narrow path. He followed the path but the tree trunk was so big the path went on and on.

Max plonked down on the path and began to cry. He was completely lost, and this tree was so big he was sure he would never get back to his parents.

"Mum, dad, where are you?"

He screamed as loud as he could. A sound, like something very big walking, came towards him.

"Max, is that you?"

The voice was his father, but it was very loud. Max looked up, and up. There was his dad towering above him.

"Dad, I'm here."

Max's dad looked down and gasped. He bent down and held out his hand. Max stepped into his father's palm, he was tiny. Somehow he had shrunk. What he thought was a giant tree was just a normal tree. His dad smiled.

"The heather. The moorland magic heather. It's made you small Max. Don't worry, the nectar of another moorland flower will turn you back to normal."

Max's dad held him carefully and they went back to mum. She picked a tiny flower and gave it to Max to drink from. The nectar was sweet. Max finished the drink and quickly began to grow back to his normal size.

"Wow, that was weird. I'm starving now."

Max squealed. His parents laughed and they all sat down to enjoy the picnic. But Max didn't go into the heather again.

Alan Smallridge

# The Necklace

Twelve-year-old skateboarder boys, Toothy and Bill, settled on the calm sandy beach of Combe Martin to hang out and relax for a couple of hours. It was already a very hot day. The sun shone fiercely, heating the golden sand like a spreading fire. The sea glimmered and shimmered and the waves were small and gentle.

Toothy stretched out on the sand and watched the villagers play in the water. Yellow sparkles of sunlight bounced off the surface of the sea dazzling him. He shaded his eyes with his hand, and it helped a little, but there was still something very bright that he couldn't block out, just on the edge of his vision.

Toothy turned his head and saw a shiny object glittering in the sand nearby. He leaned over and pulled it out. It was a beautiful diamond necklace. He showed it to Bill.

"Let me look."
Demanded Bill. Toothy handed it over and Bill held it up to his neck.

"What do you think, pretty huh?"
Toothy laughed at his friend.

His laughter turned to fear as everything went eerily silent and the light disappeared. The boys were thrown into complete darkness as night replaced day. Toothy grabbed Bill's arm pulling him to his feet.

"Wh…where are we? I can't see a thing."
He stammered.

"I don't know." Whispered Bill in a shaky voice. "But hold on."
Bill took a giant step forward. Suddenly they were falling.

The boys found themselves in an unknown place. There wasn't anything around them except a faint mysterious mist. Bill felt a rumble in his stomach, and the moment he realised he was hungry, a burrito appeared in front of him. He reached out to grab it but then they were falling again, the necklace flying from his neck.

This time they landed in a dark, gloomy gloop that had a curious shine on top. Toothy saw a stick and poked at the gloop. A small fire sprang up giving them light and warmth. In its glow they spotted the necklace gleaming on the surface of the gloop. Bill reached for it, snagged it in his fingers and held on tight.

Once again the two boys were falling. Finally, with relief, they landed back on the beach, where the sun shone hot and the sea was calm. Bill had dropped the necklace and it glittered next to them in the sand. He stretched out his hand to pick it up, his fingertips almost touching the gleaming diamonds.

"No don't!"
Shrieked Toothy.

Sam Wyborn

# Anna

Seventeen-year-old Anna was all by herself at home. Her parents were out on Moorland for the whole evening. Anna was studying for her driving test. She really wanted to pass and was working hard. The lounge was quiet, the television off, she didn't want any distractions.

Anna jumped when she heard a noise from the kitchen, a little thud. She looked up from her tablet and waited, listening, but all was silent. She went back to her studying. A few minutes passed. Anna was concentrating deeply when a loud crash came from the kitchen, followed by banging and smashing sounds. Anna jumped up and ran to the kitchen. She stopped in the doorway. Plates, cups and glasses were flying across the room, being hurled by an invisible hand.

Anna screamed. A plate hovering in the air fell to the floor. A pale figure, a ghostly figure appeared. Anna ran. She grabbed her bag and fled from the house in terror. Anna sped to her car, the one that was waiting for when she passed her driving test. At that moment, she didn't care that she shouldn't drive, she just wanted to get away from the house. Her home was right on the edge of Combe Martin, far from any other houses.

Anna jammed the keys in the ignition and turned on the engine. She gripped the steering wheel. She heard her father's words, like he was sitting next to her.

"Hold the wheel straight. Don't go too fast and look behind you when you reverse."

Anna spoke the words out loud as she backed the car out of the drive onto the road, then braked hard. In her mirror she saw a boy standing in the road. He had his hand up in front of his face. Anna opened her window and screeched.

"Are you crazy? I nearly ran you over!"
Then still filled with fear, she sped off towards Moorland. Her only thoughts were to get away from the house and get to her parents.

Anna only slowed down when she was far from her home. Moorland was just ahead and she sighed with relief when she saw her parents.

"What on earth are you doing!"
Exclaimed her mother as she pulled up beside them.

"I…I…there's…frightened."
She tried to speak.

"Calm down and tell us what happened to make you drive without a licence."
Her dad said putting his arm around her.

Anna explained to her parents what had happened at the house. She didn't think they believed her by the look on their faces. But dad told her to get in the back of the car and then he drove them home.

The three of them stepped through the back door and found the kitchen covered in broken plates, cups and glasses.

"Oh!"
Anna's mum gasped.

"There, that's where I saw the ghost."
Whispered Anna, pointing.

"Well I think it's gone now."
Replied her dad.

A bang outside made them all turn in shock. They darted from the house, and there by Anna's car, her wrecked car, stood the boy she had seen in her mirror. He was pointing at Anna. Then she knew what had happened. Her dad had told her not to drive before she got her licence. She hadn't listened. She had crashed her car into the boy and they were both dead. Her parents had been out on Moorland grieving, they were still out on Moorland grieving. She was alone. She was a ghost too.

Nicole Stevens

# Park Ring

Nine-year-old Luey sat in his classroom listening to his teacher. It was close to the end of the day and he couldn't wait. For once, his dad Bob, wasn't going to still be working when school finished. In fact, his dad Bob had taken the whole day off, and both his mum Carell and his dad had walked to school with him that morning.

Luey knew his mum had something special planned for after school. She had told him when she kissed him goodbye. He was so excited he couldn't sit still.

Carell and Bob had already enjoyed their day. They had spent it on the sunny, warm Combe Martin beach. They had a picnic and did absolutely nothing. For Bob that was a treat. As a farmer he worked long hours, especially in the summer time.

School ended and Luey ran out of the classroom. His parents were waiting for him.

"What are we doing?"
He asked excitedly.

"Well we thought we could have a barbeque on the beach."
Bob told his son. Luey's smile faded. He and Carell went to the beach nearly every day after school.

"Luey what's wrong?"
Questioned Bob.

"I think I know."
Carell replied instead.

"We go to the beach most days. What about the park?"
Luey's face lit up. They didn't go to the park very often.

"Would you like to go to the park instead Luey?"
Asked Bob. Luey nodded.

"That's settled then. Off to the park we go."
Bob told him.

The sun was shining brightly as the family strolled up the village to the park. When they got there, they found the park was empty.

"I expect everyone is at the beach."
Carell murmured. Luey grinned, he didn't mind having the whole park to themselves.

As Luey played and ran around, Bob lit the barbeque. Soon the lovely smell of cooking sausages made Luey's tummy rumble. He happily jogged up to his parents calling out.

"Is it ready? I'm starving."
Bob and Carell laughed at their son as Carell loaded a hot dog roll with sausage and tomato sauce. She handed it to Luey.

"Careful, it's very hot."
Carell warned as Luey went to take a big bite. At the same moment they all felt a rumbling under their feet. Bob grabbed his wife and son, but it was no good. The ground disappeared and they fell, all three together, down, down, into a deep hole.

The family landed with a soft thud. The floor of the hole was muddy.

"Mum, dad, where are you?"
Luey cried. It was dark and he couldn't see his parents.

"Just here Luey. Hold out your hand."
He heard his mum say. Luey did as she asked and felt her hand touch his. She pulled him towards her, and as his eyes began to get used to the dark, he saw both his parents.

"How are we going to get out?"
Luey asked. He was very scared.

Bob tugged his phone from his pocket and turned on the torch. He didn't have a signal but at least they could see.

"Don't worry Luey, we'll get out."
Bob said reassuring his son.

"What's that?"
Luey pointed to the edge of the hole. In the torch light he could see something glittering.

"Don't..."

Carell began to say, but Luey had already made a grab for it. In between his fingers was a shining diamond ring. He put it over the tip of a finger and held it up to show his parents.

"Luey!"

Bob called out and reached for him. It was too late. Luey was flying upwards.

Luey popped out of the hole and landed on the grass in the park. He jumped up and kneeled at the edge of the hole. It was dark, just a tiny glow from his dad's torch far below.

"Dad, mum, I'm ok. The ring lifted me out. I'm going to drop it in for you two. Put it on and it will lift you out too."

"Ok Luey, drop it."

He heard his dad say. Luey leaned over and let the ring fall.

"It's coming!"

He called into the hole.

Within seconds, Luey watched his mum and dad fly out of the hole. Bob's fingers were far too big for the ring, so Carell had it on and was holding tight to Bob. They landed on the grass next to Luey.

The family hugged. They were all very happy to be out of the deep dark hole.

"Let me see the ring please."

Bob said to Carell. She took it off and handed it to her husband.

"Looks like an ordinary ring to me. But there's obviously something magical about it. I can't just throw it back in because the same thing might happen to someone else."

"I bet it's a trap."

Luey said to his parents. As he spoke they heard a whispering laugh from the trees.

"Ha, ha, it's my ring, throw it back in the hole."

They couldn't see anyone, but they all heard the words.

"No, it's not funny scaring people like that."

Bob called out. He held the ring tight in his fist.

"You can't keep it."

Laughed the voice. Bob opened his hand and the ring was gone. They heard a rumbling and the hole filled in.

"Come on, let's go home."

Bob said to Carell and Luey. When they reached the park gate, Bob looked back to where the hole had been. The grass was back in place. It looked like it had when they got there.

"I think we'll stick to barbeques and playtime on the beach from now on. No more playing in this park, and there's no point warning anyone else. Who would believe us?"
He said to his family as he led them away.

Tom Bryant

# Death Bear's Cave

The night of Halloween, dad was telling his children a spooky story. Eleven-year-old John was not interested. He was too old for scary stories.

"One day in this very village, grey mist came down, the sky turned black, and five children decided to go to the Death Bear's Cave…"
John couldn't listen anymore, the story was too boring. He had heard it many times before, how the cave had swallowed the five children and they had never been seen again.

"Borrr…ring!"
Yelled John and he got up and slammed out of the house.

"I don't believe one word of it."
He muttered to himself as he plodded down the village towards the beach. With his head down, John didn't at first see the group of boys on the other side of the road.

"Oi!"
Hollered a deep voice. John looked up and his face crumbled. The voice had come from Bill the big head bully, the leader of the Golden Fury gang. The gang hated John because he was black.

The gang crossed the street heading for John. He knew he had to get away. If Bill caught him he would hurt him, like he always did. John spun around and ran. He didn't care where, just anywhere to get away from the gang. Behind him he heard shouting and knew they were chasing him.

John sped down the beach and along the walkway. He hoped he might be able to hide in the rocks, it was dark and for once the colour of his skin might help him.

"We can see you. Nowhere to go!"

Bill screeched. John darted this way and that, but the only place to escape to was Death Bear's Cave, he had to go in.

The dark walls of the cave seemed to close in as John ran into the opening.

"Not real, not real."

He chanted under his breath. He heard a laugh behind him, it was Bill and the gang.

"Told you we would get you."

He taunted as he stepped closer to John with his hands outstretched.

"No!"

Screamed John, backing down the slippery tunnel of the cave.

"Oh yes."

Grinned Bill coming closer.

With his feet slipping and sliding, John tried to escape. Then he felt nothing but air under his heel, just as Bill grabbed him. Both of them tumbled into what everyone called the Death Bear's Paw, a gaping hole in the floor of the cave. Thud, thud, bang, bang. The two boys bounced off the walls as they fell deep down, landing with a crash on a rough rocky surface.

"Now I've got you!"

Boomed a voice. Bill clung to John.

"Get me out"

He pleaded.

The hole had tunnels in both directions. From one they heard loud footsteps approaching.

"Run!"

Shouted John, pulling Bill with him down the other tunnel. Together they bolted. Their legs were pumping, their arms flailing, their eyes wide and searching. Their heartbeats echoed along the tunnel as they fled from the approaching footsteps and deep laughter.

"Ha, ha. You cannot escape me."

The voice boomed.

Panting and tiring, John pounded along the tunnel, Bill close behind. He had no idea where to go, or if they could find a way out.

"Nowhere to go!"

The voice was getting closer. Bill screamed in terror and grabbed John's shirt, knocking him off balance. John went sideways and banged into the wall. The rocks gave way and crumbled to the ground in a heap. A small hole appeared and a tiny glow of light shone out. Quickly, John yanked more rocks out of the way and the light got brighter.

Bill stood trembling by John's side, as he dragged and pulled at the wall making the hole bigger. Soon it was big enough to crawl through. John grabbed Bill and pushed him in.

"Go, move."

He told him, keeping his voice low. The boys crawled into the tunnel and scrambled along the rough floor. The light up ahead was getting brighter and brighter. Just as the tunnel opened onto the bright moonlit beach, the laugh came loud, right behind John, and something snatched his ankle.

"Bill!"

John yelled. Bill was out of the cave and turned. John was sliding backwards. Bill grasped John's outstretched hands and pulled as hard as he could. At first it didn't work, then John came flying towards him. They both landed in a heap on the sand. John scrambled up, Bill close behind, and they fled along the beach away from the cave. When they reached the path, they stopped, bending over to catch their breath.

"Th…thanks."

Panted John.

"Thank you too."

Mumbled Bill. They heard voices and looked up, scared, but it was just the rest of the gang.

"You got 'im then. We gonna pound 'im now?"

One of the gang asked. Bill shook his head.

"No, there's far worse things out there to worry about than the colour of someone's skin."

Replied Bill. The gang shrugged and frowned. John straightened up.

"I'm off home."

He said.

"See you around."

Bill replied in a friendly way.

John glanced back towards the rocks and shuddered. Yes, there were far worse things out there. His dad's story was true after all.

Jamie Martin

# Grandfather's Watch

As the sea washed upon the golden sand and skimmed the rocks, a boy named Alex was digging down into the sand of Combe Martin beach. The burning hot sun made Alex sweat, but still he persevered. Down and down he dug, changing places many times, digging and digging. Anyone watching would think the boy was just playing like other children, but Alex was afraid.

Early that morning over breakfast, Alex's mum gave him a present. It was a watch.

"Now take care of it Alex. Don't lose it whatever you do. I'm going out now, so make sure you keep that watch safe."

His mother said as she left the house. Alex wandered about the house for some time. He was bored, so he decided to go down to the beach.

It was very hot at the seaside with lots of people about, mostly families. This made Alex feel a little lonely by himself. He strolled along the walkway and stopped at the rock-pools for a while, watching other children play and laugh. He would have liked to join in, but didn't dare. He went back to the sandy beach and sat down. The people splashing about in the sea made him smile.

Alex stayed where he was for a long time. He wondered how long and glanced down at his wrist.

"Oh no."

He moaned. His watch wasn't there, he had lost it. Alex felt tears in the corners of his eyes and wiped them away. He scrambled up and retraced his footsteps, but he couldn't find the watch.

"Maybe it fell off where I was sitting. That's it, I bet it will be just on top of the sand."

He whispered to himself, as he made his way back to the beach where he had been sitting.

On his knees, Alex looked carefully around. He couldn't see the watch. That's when he began digging. He shovelled sand out of the way with his hands, but the watch was nowhere. The day passed and still Alex kept digging. Finally, as the sun dipped behind the horizon, Alex plodded home.

"Where have you been?"

Asked his mum as he walked through the door. Alex was exhausted, but he had to tell her.

"I lost the watch."

He mumbled. His mum folded her arms and frowned.

"How could you? That watch belonged to your grandfather. He asked me to give it to you when I thought you were grown up enough to look after it. Obviously you're not. Go to your room. You're grounded!"

She yelled. Alex ran from the room in tears.

A week later, Alex's mum lifted the grounding and let him go out. The first thing Alex did was go to the beach. It was a dull day and there were only a couple of people out walking their dogs. Alex found a spot on the sand and flopped down. He was still miserable about the watch.

Alex drew up his knees and wrapped his arms around them. He lowered his head and sighed. He felt a bump against his arm, then another, and then a cold wet nudge. Alex looked up into the eyes of a seal. The seal waddled around and sat in front of him.

"Hello."

Alex said very gently. The seal lowered its head and opened its mouth. Out fell the watch. The seal lifted its head, it appeared to be smiling. It let out a little bark, turned around and waddled to where the waves lapped the shore. Alex grabbed the watch and ran after the seal. He caught up to it just before it dived into the sea. The seal stopped. Alex knelt down and stroked its silky head.

"Thank you. Thank you so much."

He murmured. The seal seemed to nod before it slid into the water. Alex watched as it swam far out to sea.

Alex ran all the way home. He sped through the door and skidded to a halt in front of his mum. She looked up from her phone in surprise.

"I've got it!"

He squealed in delight, holding the watch up. His mum stood up and put her arms around him.

"Where did you find it?"
She asked.

"Well, I didn't exactly."
His mum gave him a puzzled look.

"A seal did. It brought it to me on the beach."

Alex's mum bit her lip to stop herself from laughing. She turned her head so he couldn't see the disbelief in her eyes. But Alex guessed anyway.

"Honest mum, it's true. You know, when I grow up, I want to work in one of those places where they rescue seals and release them back into the sea. One helped me, and I want to help as many as I can back."
Alex's mum hugged him. She knew her son and knew when he was telling the truth, knew she did now believe him.

Isabel Melton-Baguley

# Out Of Time

One morning a boy called Alex decided to take a stroll down to the beach in the village of Combe Martin. The street seemed very quiet, unusually quiet for the village. As he reached the beach, he could see the glimmering sea, beautiful bright sunlight bouncing from its surface. It was calm, too calm and what was most weird to Alex, no people.

Alex turned around and looked up the village. Something was wrong. The houses on both sides of the valley looked like they were rotting. Alex looked back at the beach, a little afraid. Something glittering in the sand caught his eye. He picked it up and suddenly he was in the forest overlooking the village.

Alex stood in shock. He glanced around but all he could see were big old trees. Then from the silence, he heard crying. It came from behind an enormous trunk. Alex peered around the tree and saw two identical boys. They were small, very young. Alex pushed aside his own fears, he was concerned for the boys.

"What's wrong?"

He asked in a gentle voice. The boys spoke at the same time.

"We can't get back."

They cried. Alex frowned.

"Back to our time."

They told him.

It was then Alex realised he wasn't in his own time either. Now it made sense. The rotting village, the big old trees. He had somehow been transported far into the future.

"How…how do you get back?"

Alex stammered. The boys wiped away their tears.

"At the top of the cliffs, where the sea meets the moor, there is a door. But to unlock it you must find the God's five gems. That will take us back to our own time, you too."
They told him.

"How do I find the gems?"
Alex asked. The boys looked at one another.

"We can only tell you how to find the first one. From then on you must work it out yourself."
Alex frowned.

"So why can't you get the gems then if you know that?"

"Because we are twins, and only one person can search, they must be alone."

Alex thought deeply. He wanted to help, and he wanted to get back to his own time. Before he would have thought it cool to be the only person in the village, especially in the summer when it filled up with holidaymakers, but now he realised how lonely it would be. He already missed his family.

"Tell me please."
The two boys, still talking at exactly the same time, explained that he had to go down to the beach and walk into the sea. They told him he would know what to do after that. Alex took a deep breath, turned around and jogged through the trees down to the top of the village. The street was no longer a road, just a dirt track. The houses and cottages were falling down, some just piles of stone. Alex began to run. He wanted to get down to the beach, away from the sight of the village.

The calm sea lapped the shore as Alex arrived at the beach. He wanted to run into the water but remembered what the boys had told him. He slowed to a walk and stepped into the sea. A gentle wave lifted him and pulled him under. Before his eyes was a temple. Across its door was written, Great Water Temple. Alex pushed open the door. Inside on a bed of shells rested a gemstone. Above it were the words, The Blue Sapphire of Power. Alex stretched out his hand and lifted the sapphire. He felt himself being pulled.

He was no longer in the temple, but on top of an island. It was hot and noisy. Alex looked down. He was on the edge of a fiery volcano. Something was being pushed up towards him. It flew out of the volcano and Alex held out his hand. A flaming box landed in his palm. It was so hot Alex thought he would drop it, but in an instant it cooled. On the lid Alex read, Lava Diamond.

He opened the box and inside was a beautiful orange diamond.

Alex touched it and once again found himself somewhere else. At first he thought he was back in the forest, as all around him was green. He soon realised it wasn't the trees, but green dust. On the ground Alex spotted what looked like a green rock. He bent and blew on it, the green dust floated away leaving a shining emerald, engraved with Green Emerald of Life. Alex was excited. He only had two gems to go. Quickly he picked the emerald up.

Alex felt water under his feet. He looked down, worried he was back in the sea, and sighed with relief when he saw he was standing in a large puddle. The water shimmered and flashed. Alex stared at it, it seemed to be moving. Then he realised it was something under the water that was flashing. He bent down and saw a sliver of silver. He could just make out its markings, Lightning Bolt. Alex knew it was the fourth gem and lifted it from the water. Glittering crystals flashed and Alex was once more transported.

Alex found himself standing where the moor met the sea. In front of him right on the edge of the cliff was the door. It sparkled with coloured gems, blue, green, orange, silver and red. He was not alone. The twins stood next to him.

"If we're all here, you must have the gems."
Said the twins. Alex shook his head.

"But I only have four…"
He paused, pushing his hand into his pocket. He pulled out the first object he had seen shining in the sand. In his palm was a big bright red gem.

"That's it. The Great Master Ruby."
Squealed the twins.

"Give the gems to the door."
They told him excitedly. Alex held all five gems out and they flew to the door, joining the other glittering stones. The door opened and Alex and the twins were sucked through.

Alex was on his own beach in his own time. The sea was calm and the day sunny, but it was busy. Families were playing and having fun. Alex took a deep breath of relief. He was home. He felt a little sad too, as he wondered and hoped the twins were back where they belonged.


Joshua Woodger

# Stolen Silver

One very foggy morning, two twelve-year-old boys, Bob and Jimey went for a walk down to the beach. The sea was rough, the waves crashing against the rocks and rolling over the sand.

For a while the boys dodged the incoming tide as they threw pebbles into the water, making them skip across the waves.

"Look Bob, there's something shining."
Jimey called out to his friend. Bob dropped the pebble he was about to throw and looked where Jimey pointed. He could see the shiny thing poking out of the sand. A wave washed over it and cleared more sand. Both boys could now see it was a gleaming bracelet.

"I wonder if it's worth something."
Jimey said reaching for the bracelet. Bob put his hand out at the same time and they touched it together.

The boys suddenly found themselves on a ledge. The sea was below them, the cliffs reaching up far above them and a small cave opening behind them.

"How did we get here?"
Bob squeaked in a scared voice.

"I don't know. But let's get off the ledge."
Jimey replied pulling him into the cave.

The cave was dark with a narrow tunnel leading into the rocks. The two boys slowly made their way down the tunnel. It was damp and quiet. Little drips of water tapping on the rocks was the only sound they heard for some time.

Deeper and deeper they went. The tunnel seemed to go on forever.

"Maybe we should go back."
Bob whispered.

"I think so."
Replied Jimey, turning around. Just then they heard a bang, then another, like hammering. The floor of the cave gave way and they dropped. They landed in another cave, much bigger than the first one. The walls were shining, just like the bracelet.

"Give us back our silver."
A voice boomed. Bob and Jimey grabbed each other in terror.

"Give us our silver and we will let you go."
The voice bellowed again.

"Th…the bracelet."
Stammered Jimey to Bob. Bob still clasped the bracelet in his hand. He held it up and threw it at the wall. The bracelet stuck to the wall.

"Long ago the villagers of Combe Martin stole our silver. But you have given some of it back. Now you can go."
The voice spoke, not so loudly.

"But…how?"
Bob asked. As soon as he spoke the boys found themselves back on the beach. The fog had gone, the sea was calm and the sun was shining.

"Is this a dream?"
Bob asked Jimey.

"No, but I don't think I'm going to tell anyone. No one would believe us. I do know that I won't pick up anything the sea washes up ever again."
Jimey replied.

"Neither will I."
Bob said with a shudder.


Ruaridh Bailey

# Amber

Just like any other morning Amber got up from bed. She went downstairs and outside. She lived on a farm and her job was to feed the animals. She entered the barn and tipped out the feed. Her dog was by her side, and next she would walk and play with him as she did every day.

Amber ran from the barn and through the gate into the fields. She expected to see her dog running along with her, but he was still back at the barn. Amber shrugged and thought he might have spotted one of the farm cats to chase. She left him to it and went for a stroll across the farmland.

Later, Amber returned to her house. It was very quiet and no one was home. She didn't know where her family were, and felt annoyed they had gone out without her. All day she waited, but they didn't come home. Angrily, Amber went to bed. She tried to read her book for a while but she was so tired she fell asleep.

In the morning Amber climbed from bed and went downstairs. No one was about, so she thought it must be very early. She was still cross with her family, so didn't go and wake any of them. She went outside to the barn, and was surprised to see the animal feed she had put out hadn't been touched. She looked about for her dog. He was sleeping in the hay. She called him but he didn't come to her.

Amber stomped back to the house, first her family, now her dog. As she passed the fireplace she saw cards, lots of cards, on the mantelpiece. She frowned, thinking she had missed someone's birthday, and that was maybe why her family had gone off without her the day before.

Amber heard a car pull up outside. She smiled, her family were home, they hadn't left her. She ran to meet them, but they ignored her.

"Mum, what's wrong? What have I done?"

Her mum walked past her without a word. Amber rushed into the house and up the stairs to her room. She was upset, in tears. This wasn't fair, she hadn't done anything wrong. She heard her brother come up. He stopped in her doorway and looked at her.

"What?"

She said. But he turned away without a word. Amber was stunned. Why were they treating her like this?

Amber fled from her room in tears. She ran down the stairs, determined to find out what she had done that was so wrong. Her parents were standing by the fire. They looked so sad. Her dad had his arm around her mum and they were both looking at the cards. Amber strode over to them and reached out to her mum. As she touched her, her mum shivered. Amber looked up at the big mirror that hung over the fire and gasped. She could see the reflection of her parents, just her parents, not herself.

It all came back to Amber in a rush. Suddenly she could see what was on the cards, they were all words of sympathy. No wonder the animals didn't eat their food, no wonder her dog didn't come when he was called. Nobody had left her by herself, she had left them all, she was dead.

Bonnie Turner

# Old Man's Tale

An old man in Martin's Combe, claimed many times over the years, he had seen glimpses of a ghost pirate. No one believed him except Jake and Oscar, two best friends who loved any pirate stories. This led them to quite an adventure.

One afternoon, Jake's dad came home from his shift at the police station. He was grumpy, and complained that the old man had been into the station to report seeing a ghost pirate. This caught Jake's attention. He immediately phoned Oscar.

"Should we try and find this pirate ghost?"
He asked his friend excitedly.

"Let's go out on the kayak this evening."
Suggested Oscar.

The evening sun shone, an orange ball on the horizon, and a chilly wind whistled around the bay. The unusually still sea shimmered in the last rays of light. Once the sun had settled for its long sleep, creatures disappeared and silence triumphed. Even the wind faded.

Jake and Oscar pushed their kayak into the sea. They were nervous but excited, as they set out with hopes of discovering the mysterious ghost. Darkness fell as they quietly paddled out of the bay. The only movement on the still sea was the ripples the boys made as they cut through the water.

Following the overshadowing cliffs, the boys rested for a while near Camel's Eye, sheltering from the open ocean. Here, away from all unnatural light, the stars shone, reflecting in the clear water, creating a never ending galaxy. Then, from the darkness, they saw the most amazing sight, a ship. It was old, very old. Tatty, torn sails flapped, there were gaping holes in its sides, and water dripped from its rotting deck as it emerged, as if resurrected from the depths of the ocean, long forgotten for centuries. It was a pirate ship, a ghostly pirate ship.

The ship drew the boys, bewitching them. They rowed to it and hauled themselves out of the kayak, up onto its battered deck. From all around, they felt eyes watching them, but couldn't see anyone. Suddenly, Oscar tripped. Jake helped his friend to his feet and as they straightened, a net dropped. They were trapped, the heavy weight knocking them unconscious.

When they awoke, they found themselves tied tightly to the mast. From the darkness, faces began to emerge. Horrors from the blackest hell surrounded them, they were the dead faces of ghost pirates. In that moment, Jake and Oscar knew the old man's stories were true.

Trapped and tied, they wondered how they could escape this nightmare. Then Oscar remembered he had his fishing knife with him, and hoped the ghouls hadn't found it.

"In my pocket, my knife. Can you reach it?"
He whispered to Jake. Jake wriggled around and found the knife. Carefully, so the ghost pirates didn't notice, Jake began to cut the foul ropes holding his friend's wrists. Oscar came free and did the same for Jake.

The two boys jumped to their feet. Slipping and sliding across the ship's deck, they dived into the cold deep water and swam to their kayak. Frantically they rowed, until they felt their hearts would explode, as distant cackles of laughter echoed across the ocean.

Sliding the kayak onto the beach, the boys raced to the nearby police station. Wet and very out of breath, they gabbled out their tale.

"There, there, don't worry, I will sort everything out."
The constable comfortingly told them, as he ran his tongue over the edge of his golden tooth and smiled wickedly.

Faith Broxholme

# Picture Of Mist

All was calm in Combe Martin, it was just like any other day. The sun was shining and the land was green. High above the bay, rocky cliffs met the rolling hills of Exmoor and everything seemed just perfect.

The villagers were out and about enjoying the beautiful day, doing all the things they usually did. Nobody thought anything was wrong. Nobody noticed that some of the villagers were no longer in the village. Well, people did move, most thought, when they did realise someone had gone, but didn't really think much about it.

Quite often, thick mist would roll in off the sea and wrap itself around the village. That was normal too for a seaside village. But this day, someone did notice something odd about the mist. Lilly was waiting for her mum outside the shop at seaside, when she saw the mist begin to creep across the top of the cliffs. She watched as it slid down towards the beach and out to sea. It seemed to form a wall surrounding the village.

"Mum look at this."

Lilly called out as she saw her mum coming out of the shop. Lilly's mum looked at where Lilly was pointing and stared in surprise. Other villagers began to notice the two of them and looked too. The mist was hovering all about them but wasn't coming any closer.

"What's that?"

Yelled one of the villagers. Everyone looked. The mist was changing. It went from dark and grey to bright and colourful. The shape of it altered too. The edges began to straighten, framing the scene, forming a picture.

The villagers watched in wonder as the they saw small dark figures moving about in the picture. They couldn't make them out. Then one of the figures came closer. It was a girl. She came right to the edge of the picture and stopped.

"That's Rose!"
Lilly cried out. She ran forward but her mum grabbed her.

"No Lilly, don't go closer. Look you can just see the frame around the edge. Somehow Rose is in a picture and I bet those other figures are villagers too. The mist has taken them, you must stay away, it's very dangerous."

Lilly, her mum and the other villagers backed away in fear. The picture began to fade and the mist disappeared out to sea.

"Mum I only saw Rose an hour ago. She was going up onto the moor for a walk. What if the mist took her then?"
Lilly said to her mum as they quickly walked home.

"There's nothing we can do Lilly. We just have to stay away from the mist when it comes, now we know what happens."

When they reached home, Lilly went to her room. She wanted to be alone to think. She had seen her friend just over an hour ago. Then the mist came, but it didn't come down into the village. It didn't take anyone from the village, so it must only take them when they're on the moor. She had an idea. What if the mist took an hour to make a picture? Maybe if someone knew that they could go in and get the people out.

Lilly crept out of the house, she knew her mum wouldn't let her go and try out her plan. She climbed up the cliff path and onto open moorland. Exmoor spread out before her, green and beautiful. Lilly stopped, waited and watched. In the distance she spotted a faint mist drifting towards her. Still she waited. When the mist was close enough to touch, Lilly checked her watch and stepped into it.

For a long time, she was surrounded by thick fog, then as she carried on walking she stepped into bright sunshine.

"Lilly!"
Someone called. Lilly turned and saw her friend Rose running towards her. There were other people too.

"You went into the mist didn't you?"
Sobbed Rose.

"Yes, but I know how to get out."
She replied looking at her watch.

"Quick, everyone. We have to hurry. It takes the mist an hour to make a new picture. It's nearly been that long. If we all go now we can get back out

of the mist and home."
Lilly called out. She took Rose by the hand and led her back into the mist, the others following.

Lilly, Rose and the other lost villagers stepped out of the mist onto the top of the cliffs with one minute to spare. Lilly sighed with relief, her idea had worked. She ran home and told her mum, who was very angry with her, but very proud too. They spread the news around the village, and from then on no one ever went into the mist again.

Grace Seldon

# Haunted Cave

"Are we there yet?" Ten-year-old Libby called to her dad from the back of the car.

"How many more times Libby? We're not in Combe Martin yet." Katrina, Libby's older sister grumbled.

"Actually, the village is just ahead." Said their dad, making Libby squeal with delight. It had been a very long journey. First the tiring flight from Australia, then the lengthy car drive from the airport, to finally reach the village they hadn't seen for many years.

Combe Martin was their real home, even though Libby didn't remember it. She had moved with her family to Australia when she was very little. Now they had come back to be near her gran who was getting old. The only one in the family who wasn't happy to be back was fifteen-year-old Katrina.

"Oh joy." Mumbled Katrina, burying her face in the book she was reading. Libby ignored her, she wouldn't let her sister spoil her excitement.

The family arrived at gran's house and Libby leapt from the car. The house was on the cliffs and overlooked the bay below. It was a beautiful sunny day, warm with the sparkling sea splashing the rocks at the foot of the cliffs. Katrina slowly got out of the car and sulkily plodded into the house.

The next morning Libby wanted to go out and explore. Her parents had so much to do getting settled in they told Katrina to take her.

"Take me to the cave please Katrina. The one I read about in my book." Katrina huffed and stomped off out of the house, Libby following, her little book tucked tight in her pocket. It was a pocket book of myths and legends of Combe Martin and Libby had read it over and over again.

Katrina led Libby down the cliff path to the beach, along the walkway, and across the rocks to the cave. She remembered the way quite well, remembered the cave, the beach and the cliffs, and began to feel a little less grumpy.

"Well here it is Libby. Do you want to go in?"
Katrina asked. Libby nodded excitedly and climbed up to the cave.

The entrance was dark and a little scary, but Libby was determined to go in. With Katrina close behind her, Libby slowly and carefully made her way deeper into the cave. It got darker and darker and curved this way and that.

"How far does it go?"
Libby whispered to her sister.

"I don't know. Maybe we should go back."
Katina said, trying not to sound nervous.

Libby agreed and the two girls turned around to head back the way they had come. They walked and walked but there was no sign of the opening.

"I think we're lost."
Cried Libby, flopping to the cold wet floor of the cave. Katrina knelt and hugged her sister.

"We will find the way out Libby. Don't cry."

"No you won't."
Came a deep voice from all around them. Libby screamed.

"It's the man, the man from my book Katrina. He's bad. He's going to hurt us, the book says so."
A small glow from ahead grew as it got closer. It bounced up and down. The girls held each other tight in fear as they watched. A figure appeared behind the light. It was a very old man with long white hair and beard. He was smiling.

"I won't hurt you. But what I said is true. You won't find the way out alone."
His voice was soft and gentle.

"Who are you?"
Muttered Libby.

"I'm the keeper of the caves, and I help children who get lost in them find their way out."

"But my book says you haunt the caves and take the children away."
Muttered Libby. The old man smiled, but his eyes looked sad.

"Sometimes, I can't get to them in time. Sometimes, the tide reaches them first, then they're gone. But not today. Today I have found you two before the sea. So follow me and I will show you the way out."

Libby and Katrina followed the old man and his light along the winding paths of the cave. They never would have found the way out alone. When the entrance of the cave could be seen up ahead, the old man stopped.

"There, see the sun shining in? That's the way out. Goodbye Libby, goodbye Katrina."

He said softly and disappeared. Libby stared at the spot with her mouth open.

"How did he know our names?"

"I don't know. But let's get out of here Libby, and next time we come here we won't go so far in."

Libby and Katrina climbed out of the cave, back along the walkway and up the cliff path home. They rushed into the house and gabbled out to their parents what had happened in the cave. Mum and dad listened and smiled, but the girls could see they thought they had imagined it all. Gran though, gave them a look that told them she knew exactly what had happened.

Lucy Woolmington

# The Statue

Winter was coming. Icy wind rippled the moorland grass overlooking the sparkling sea of Combe Martin bay. Crisp, cold air stung the faces of the villagers as they gathered together on the beach. Twelve-year-old John and Clio were amongst them. They were taking part in a beach clean. The high tide had washed all sorts of rubbish onto the sand, and the villagers were ready with bags and grab sticks to clear it away.

John and Clio wandered off by themselves, to a spot of beach where no one else was cleaning. They began to collect the plastic bottles and bags scattered about. John spotted something sticking out of the sand. He called Clio over and they bent to look. Clio pushed the sand away and saw a small statue buried in the sand. She tugged it and it came free.

Clio held it up for John to see. It was very dirty, grey and dull. John held his gloved hand out and Clio put the statue in his palm. Using his other hand, John rubbed the statue, cleaning the sand off with his glove. As it came clean they saw it was covered in tiny pieces of sparkling rock.

"Wow!"
Exclaimed Clio. John held the spectacular little statue closer, he could see something written on it.

"There's a date on it."
He told Clio. Clio peered at the statue too.

"Maybe it's really old. We should take it to the museum."
She said excitedly.

"We can't. It's nearly winter. The museum isn't open, and…" He paused and looked closer. "It's not old. At least the date isn't. Oh…"
John frowned.

"What is it"

Clio whispered.

"The date. It's a hundred years in the future."

John gasped dropping the statue in shock.

As the tiny statue hit a rock, it split open, and inside the two children saw a glimmering shiny diamond. Clio reached out and touched the diamond with a finger. Suddenly everything changed. They were on an island in the middle of a calm blue sea. There was nothing but water all around them. It was very hot and the only shelter was a palm tree.

John and Clio were afraid. They dragged their winter coats and gloves off and sat under the tree.

"What are we going to do John?"

Asked Clio, close to tears.

"Where's the statue?"

John replied. Clio looked around her. The sand was pure white and soft as silk. It flowed through her fingers like water.

"I can't see it. Did it even come with us?"

She said. John stood up and kicked at the sand.

"Ouch!"

He yelled, hopping around. He had stubbed his foot on something hard in the sand. Clio dragged at the sand until she found what John had kicked. It was the statue.

"John, it's the statue. And look at the date."

John stopped hopping around and peered at the statue. He could just make out the date on it, their date.

"Bang it against the tree. See if it will open."

Clio jumped up and slammed the statue into the tree trunk. It sprung open and inside was the gleaming diamond.

"Touch it John."

She squealed. John did as she asked and suddenly they were back on their beach. The statue was by their side. It was dull and grey again.

"Leave it there."

John cried.

"Don't touch it again."

"We can't. Suppose someone else finds it and the same thing happens to them."

Replied Clio.

"What have you got there?"
A very old man asked. The children didn't know his name, only that he was the oldest resident in the village.
"Uh, um…"
John and Clio said together. They didn't want the old man to touch the statue, and they didn't think he would believe them if they said why.
"It's all right. I know what it is."
The old man said with a wrinkled smile. He picked the statue up.
"It's time. It showed you an island in the future, because you are so young, but for me, it will take me back to the past, I can be young again."
The old man tapped the statue on the rocks and it opened. He touched its bright diamond centre. John and Clio watched as he slowly began to fade, his face getting younger He waved, smiled and disappeared, leaving John and Clio to wonder if it had all really happened.

Bonar Thwaites

# The Wooden Chest

Isobel and Bob decided to take their two children, Grace and Sam, to the beach for the day. It was a lovely warm sunny day. With all their swimming suits and a picnic packed up, the family strolled down to Combe Martin bay and settled on the sand.

Bob and Isobel laid on their towels and the children happily played in the sand. Sam was digging. He filled bucket after bucket with sand and his hole got bigger and bigger. Grace used the sand from Sam's hole to make a sandcastle. She was just on her way back from the water when she heard her brother shout. Grace ran to Sam as their parents sat up wondering what had happened.

"Look, mum, dad, Grace!"
Sam squealed. The family looked into the hole where Sam was pointing. They could see the top of a wooden chest.

Bob leaned into the hole and pushed more sand out of the way. There was a handle on top of the chest. Bob grabbed it and pulled. He tugged and yanked, and finally the chest came free from the sand. Bob hauled it onto the beach. The wood looked very old. There was a dull rusty clasp and heavy hinges.

"Let me. I found it."
Moaned Sam. He grabbed the clasp and lifted it. The lid squealed as it opened. Inside the chest the family saw a pile of rubbish. There were empty bottles and sweet papers, chip wrappers and plastic cups.

"Oh that's nasty and smelly."
Cried Grace. Bob tried to slam the lid, but the rubbish grew and grew and overflowed the chest onto the beach.

"What are we going to do dad?"
Grace screamed.

"We have to collect all the rubbish and put it back."
Bob told her.

"Hurry, we have to put it in faster than it's coming out."

The family dashed about gathering up the rubbish, stuffing it back into the chest. They were quick, and soon the chest stopped dumping more rubbish onto the beach.

"This chest must be magic. Somehow it collects the rubbish that gets thrown into the sea and left on the beach. We will have to close it up and bury it deep where it won't get dug up again."
Bob said to his family.

"Maybe we should take it out to sea and drop it in the water. That way it will stay hidden."
Suggested Isobel. Bob nodded in agreement.

"I'll borrow Arthur's boat."

The family loaded the chest onto Arthur's boat and sailed far out. When all they could see of the village was a tiny speck, they dropped the chest over the side. It sank. All four of them watched until it disappeared beneath the water.

"Let's go home. It's been a long and busy day. Tomorrow we will come back to the beach, but just don't dig so far down next time Sam."
Bob said as he sailed them back to shore.

"I won't dad. I want to play in the sand not cover it in rubbish."
Sam replied grinning.

Lacey Bowden-Broadley

# Seashell

Sam and Josh went down to the beach in Combe Martin. It was a lovely, bright sunny day. The sea was calm with small waves rippling to the shore. With the warmth of the sun on their backs, Sam and Josh strolled along the walkway to the rock pools.

"Let's catch some crabs."
Said Sam. Josh agreed and for some time the two boys enjoyed dipping their lines into the rock pools, getting excited when the crabs took the bait.

Neither boy noticed the day going by, or the sky getting darker, until big drops of rain splashed onto their heads.

"Oh, it's raining!"
Exclaimed Josh.

"Come on. We can go into the cave until it stops."
Sam replied, pulling their lines out of the water.

The rain was getting heavier and the sky darker, as the boys jogged to the cave. They climbed up the rocks and stepped into the dark mouth of the cave. The rain swept in on a strong wind.

"We need to get further inside."
Josh said, leading the way down the tunnel. Sam followed. It was quite exciting going deeper into the dark creepy cave. The walls were wet and the floor slippery, but it was better than being outside in the rain.

Deep inside the rocky cliff, the boys heard rumbling thunder. It echoed up the tunnel and lightning lit the entrance far behind them.

"Wow, that's a big storm out there."
Sam stated.

"Sam, my feet are getting wet."

Moaned Josh. Sam bent down. The cave floor wasn't just wet anymore. It was filling up with water.

"We're going to get trapped!"
Screeched Sam. He grabbed Josh's arm and pulled him even further into the cave.

Up ahead he could see something bright and hoped it was another way out. But when they reached it, he saw it was a shiny seashell stuck to the cave wall.

"Oh, I thought it was a way out." He mumbled to Josh. "But it's just an old seashell shining."

"Look Sam, it's getting bigger."
Squealed Josh. The seashell was growing and getting brighter. As it got bigger it dropped from the wall into the rising water.

"Quick, get in."
Josh shouted over the storm.

The two boys climbed into the shell. It glowed even more brightly and began to float further into the cave. The water rushed in behind them as they bounced along. Suddenly, they burst from the cave into the sea. The shell took them far out away from the storm. Then it stopped.

Josh and Sam could see Combe Martin. The storm pounded the beach and the village but they were safe on the edge of it. They watched as the storm finally blew itself out. The seashell began to float again, towards the beach. As it reached the shore it began to shrink. Josh and Sam climbed out onto the sand and watched as the shell got smaller and smaller. It then disappeared under the water.

The beach was a mess. The storm had washed up seaweed, pebbles and driftwood and washed away a lot of sand. Many villagers were busy repairing it. Josh and Sam joined in. They kept their little adventure to themselves, after all who would believe them?


Rhys Atkinson

# Princess Polo

Princess Polo is the richest fish in the world. This is because she is a star in the movies under the ocean. One day as she was polishing her scales and looking at her reflection in her beautiful stained glass mirror, she saw behind her a shark.

"Hmm, I know that shark. He's a so called villain."
She murmured to herself. Princess Polo flicked her tail and fins and went to meet the shark. She wasn't afraid, no sea creature would dare harm her, she was too famous.

Princess Polo swam boldly up to the shark. The shark opened his mouth showing his sharp gleaming teeth.

"Why did the chicken go to MacDonald's to get fried?"
He spurted out on a laugh. Princess Polo wasn't amused.

"Ha, Ha, very funny. You're no villain are you? What's your name?"
The shark frowned, trying to look serious and scary, but it didn't fool Princess Polo.

"Well?"
She questioned. The shark sighed.

"My name is Racknos, and no I'm not a villain. I'm not bad at all and I don't want to be. I just want to make people laugh, not scare them. But everyone thinks I am bad and that I can keep the even more bad creatures away, but I can't, I don't know how."

Princess Polo felt sorry for Racknos. She thought for a moment.

"I have an idea."
She told him, beckoning with her fin. She led him to her studio. There she introduced him to one of her actor friends, and in a huddle made a plan.

Later that day, Racknos was hanging out at the Sea Café trying to entertain some of the younger fish. They didn't trust Racknos, they thought he wanted to eat them. But they were even more afraid when they heard a squelching noise outside the café. Racknos got up to see what it was, the little fish following behind. What they saw terrified them. It was a giant squid, and they knew it would definitely eat them.

Racknos blocked the door and told the little fish to stay inside. Then he boldly went out to confront the squid. The huge squid laughed at Racknos.

"You don't scare me. I'm going to eat the whole kingdom."
Racknos opened his mouth wide and displayed every one of his razor sharp teeth. Like a bullet he swam at the squid and closed his mouth over one of its tentacles. Racknos bit down, not hard enough to bite through, just enough to sting. The squid howled with pain. Racknos let go and the squid spun around and fled from the kingdom.

Racknos heard a great cheer behind him. He looked back and saw all the sea creatures from the kingdom clapping and smiling. Princess Polo was amongst them. Standing by her side was her actor friend, he was holding a squid mask. Racknos gulped as he realised he had chased away a real giant squid.

Princess Polo swam to Racknos' side. Everyone stopped and stared at her beauty, ready to listen to what she had to say.

"Now you can all see Racknos is not bad or a villain. He doesn't want to hurt any of you. All he wants to do is make you laugh and have fun. But he is brave and will protect you when you need him to."
She announced. Racknos blushed. He wasn't used to being praised.

For the first time ever Racknos discovered he had many friends and he was happy. Princess Polo made him even happier when she bought him a joke shop, the one thing he had always wanted. From then on, Racknos entertained the kingdom, protected it too, now he knew he could.

Samuel Young

# Beach Clean

The big storm over Combe Martin had finally finished. Rocks had fallen down from the cliffs and enormous logs had been washed up by the clashing sea. The beach was wrecked. Sand had been dragged away from the entrance to the beach and there was rubbish everywhere.

It was quite usual for this to happen to the village, and as usual a large group of villagers joined together on the beach to clear it up. Two boys, Jack and Daniel, were amongst the crowd. They always liked to help put their beach back together again.

"Oh that's not good!"
Shouted one of the villagers. The boys looked in the direction he was pointing. The hut where the clean-up equipment was kept was in bits. The storm had pulled it apart.

"And look, the storm is coming back in!"
Yelled another villager.

Everyone stared out across the sea. The waves were getting bigger and thick black clouds were rolling in towards them. The wind began to howl as the water crashed to the shore, dragging more of the beach away. Pulling their hoods up and their coats close, the villagers ran from the storm.

Jack and Daniel were on the walkway. Waves like huge sea monsters smashed onto the path, cutting them off. The only place they could go to for safety was the cave.

"We should be safe here."
Gasped Jack.

"I don't know. Look the storm is breaking up the walkway."
Daniel said backing further into the cave, Jack following.

All around them they could hear the booming storm echoing off the walls of the cave. The floor was getting wetter as the sea flooded in.

"We're trapped."

Cried Jack. He backed right up against the cave wall. As he put his hands behind him, he felt something drop into his palm. It felt cold and hard.

"Daniel, shine your phone here."

He told his friend, holding out his hand. Daniel did as he asked. Between his fingers was a big old-fashioned key.

"Where did that come from?"

Asked Daniel. Jack shrugged.

"It fell out of the wall. Hey, look."

In the light of the torch the two boys could see a keyhole in the cave wall. Jack reached forward and put the key into it. It fitted exactly. Jack turned the key and there was a loud noise. The wall opened. Jack and Daniel heard a sucking sound. The water on the floor was being pulled into the gap and the noise of the storm had stopped.

For a moment Jack and Daniel were too surprised to move. Then the wall closed and the keyhole was gone. So was the key. Quickly they sped down the tunnel to the cave entrance. When they got there they saw bright sunshine. The walkway was back in one piece and the beach was clean. The sand was soft and dry and back where it should be. The storm was gone, the sea calm and the sky blue.

"Wow, somehow we did this."

Jack grinned. Daniel nodded, a big smile on his face too.

"Yes we did, but I'm not sure I want to get stuck in that cave again."

He replied.

"But I suppose if we had to do it again to save our beach, we would."

He continued. Jack laughed.

"Yes, but not today. Come on let's get an ice-cream."

Kyran Bird

# Never Ending Love

There was once a girl called Anna Merryweather. She was sixteen and very much in love with her boyfriend. She squabbled a lot with her mother about this, and one stormy day on the thirteenth of July, Anna stomped off to the beach after one of those quarrels. The water was rough and dark, the waves big and strong.

Worrying about the argument, Anna strolled too near to the sea and a sudden wave swept her off her feet and dragged her in. When her mum realised she hadn't come home, a search party set out to find her, but there was no sign of Anna.

Caleb was Anna's boyfriend. He was smart and shy. He didn't have many friends and was an easy target for the local bullies, especially now Anna was gone. To Keep out of their way, Caleb wandered along the beach every day hoping to find Anna. Every day he searched and searched, salty tears sliding down his cheeks, dropping to the sand to join the salty sea.

Two years later, on the thirteenth of July, Caleb finally found Anna. Her body washed up on the shore. It was the most horrifying sight he had ever seen, and frightened him so much he was terrified of going to the beach again.

From then on the villagers believed that part of the beach was haunted. Many of them said they had seen the ghost of Anna wandering along the water's edge. Some said they heard her crying out for Caleb. But Caleb would never go there.

Eventually, Caleb began to feel less and less miserable about Anna. He met a girl called Liss. She was new to the village, they started going out, and she didn't know about Anna. She only knew the rumours of a ghost haunting part of the beach.

One evening Caleb was on his way home. He still watched out for bullies even though they weren't as bad now, but he did still avoid the beach, that fear had not gone away. Suddenly Liss jumped out from behind a wall making him jump.

"Hey, what are you doing? You scared me."
Caleb gasped. Liss laughed.

"I'm changing our date."
She giggled.

"Go and get changed and meet me up at the carpark."
Caleb agreed and he jogged off home. He had no idea what Liss had planned and he was quite excited.

Caleb changed into his best jeans and shirt, grabbed his wallet and set off to meet Liss. She was waiting for him in the carpark, in a car.

"Where did you get that?"
Caleb asked.

"I passed my test today. I didn't tell you in case I failed. Mum and dad gave me the car for passing. Come on, get in, we're going for a drive."
She replied. Caleb jumped in the car and Liss drove off. They didn't go far.

"Uh, what are we doing here?"
Caleb asked nervously. Liss had stopped the car by the wall overlooking the haunted part of the beach.

"For fun. Come on Caleb. Let's go and find the village ghost."
Without waiting for him, Liss sped off down the path to the beach. Caleb slowly got out of the car and followed, telling himself it was about time he got over his fear. He could see Liss at the edge of the calm water. She had her shoes off and was splashing about. Caleb walked faster. He began to feel more confident. Just as he reached Liss, an enormous wave came from nowhere and dragged Liss into the sea.

"No!"
Screamed Caleb. Then a voice came from behind him.

"You have forgotten about me. You left me."
Caleb spun around and saw the ghost of Anna. He was terrified.

"N…no I didn't. I loved you and I…I searched for you…"
Caleb stammered.

"Then come with me now. If you do, I can save her."
Anna whispered, pointing to where Liss was struggling in the raging water.

Caleb knew he had no choice. He couldn't let another girl drown and become a ghost to haunt him. He held out his hand to Anna. As he touched her icy fingers, all the love he had for her came flooding back to him. She was his one true love. Anna led him into the cold swirling sea. The waves lifted up and covered his head. As he went down he saw Liss being carried by the water onto the beach, to safety. Caleb relaxed and let the sea take him. Anna was with him. Finally, they were together as it should have always been. Finally, he was happy and free from fear.

Morgan Wakenell

# The Shapeshifter

The sun was shining brightly over Combe Martin. Out in the bay, Jack, a very friendly shark, was swimming about, enjoying the sun shining down on the warm sea. It was a perfect day, at first. But as Jack swam near to the surface he saw the sky darken above. Day had suddenly turned into night.

Jack dived under the sea. He thought he knew what had happened and had to do something about it. As Jack swam deeper, the water became darker, but Jack knew exactly where he was going to, the temple.

The tall stone temple rose from the bottom of the sea. Jack swam inside and made his way to the centre, where he hoped to find the great amulet of time. He believed it was the amulet that had turned the day back into night, but he didn't know why it had happened. The amulet was only ever used by the sea creatures to change time when something had gone wrong.

Jack saw the glow of the amulet and quickly swam to it. The amulet was where it should be, on its rocky bed in the middle of the temple. But just as Jack reached it, the rock changed. It became a huge monster with glowing eyes. Jack flicked his fins and swam away from it in fear. The monster was the terrible shapeshifter, and it had taken the amulet of time.

Jack was fast, faster than the shapeshifter. He flicked his big body from side to side and escaped the monstrous creature, up through the temple to a place he knew had a secret opening. Once inside he turned around and watched the shapeshifter on the other side searching for him. Jack knew he couldn't stay hidden, he had to get the amulet back, or time would keep on changing back and forward.

Jack waited for a while. Eventually the shapeshifter got tired of looking for him and turned into a small blue fish. As it darted about Jack noticed the orange spot on one of its fins. It was the same colour as its eyes had been as the monster. It was also the same colour as the amulet of time.

Jack knew what he had to do. He didn't want to because he was a friendly shark, and never hurt any of the sea creatures, but this shapeshifter was dangerous. Jack waited until the shapeshifter swam closer, then closer to the secret opening. Then Jack sprang forward. He opened his huge mouth and closed it over the fish. The shapeshifter tried to change inside his mouth, but it was trapped. As it wiggled and shifted, it dropped the amulet. Jack felt the great amulet of time drop onto his tongue, free from the shapeshifter. Jack knew if he opened his mouth the shapeshifter would escape and turn back into a monster. So he did the only thing he could think of, he swallowed it.

Jack swam back to the centre of the temple. He opened his mouth and the amulet of time dropped back onto its rock. It glowed brightly, lighting up the temple. Jack flicked his tail and his fins and swam out of the temple back to the surface. He reached the bay of Combe Martin and saw sunlight sparkling above him. Time was where it should be and the shapeshifter was gone forever.

Joshua Bulloch

# Undersea House

Once there were two boys, Ben and Frank. They loved the sea and spent a lot of time playing in the beautiful waters of Combe Martin bay. Both were excellent swimmers and often dived deep under the water, even when the sea was rough and the waves were big.

One morning, very early, a storm woke Ben. The sound of the howling wind drew him to his bedroom window. As he looked through the glass he could see the trees on the edge of the cliffs fighting the wind. Below, he could just make out the peaks of white churning waves crashing to shore.

Ben was excited. He loved the sea when it was so busy. Hurriedly he pulled on his wetsuit and swim shoes and crept from the house. He knew he should call his best friend Frank, but Frank really didn't like being woken up so early. Instead he decided to go for a swim alone and tell Frank about it later.

Ben stood on the beach watching the waves as the sun began to rise above the horizon. Glimmering light washed over the sea, calming the salty water. Ben stepped forward and dived into it. At first the cold took his breath, but as he raised his head above the waves he breathed fresh air and felt free.

Ben swam far out. After sometime he stopped and dived down. The deeper he went, the darker the water became. But Ben was not afraid. He had dived deep many times. Flipping over in the water, Ben could just make out the shimmer of light above. He looked back down and got a surprise. Below him was a house, not a wooden shack like the ones that sometimes got washed out to sea, but a real solid house with a door and windows.

Ben was very curious. In the silent depths of the sea he gazed at the door, paused for a moment, then swam towards it. As he touched the door it opened, so Ben swam inside. There was furniture and all the usual items found inside any house. Ben couldn't believe what he was seeing. Even more mysterious was that he didn't have to hold his breath anymore. Ben knew he just had to go and get Frank and show him the house.

Ben emerged from the sea onto a beach bright with sunlight. It was warm, the sun high in the sky. It didn't seem like he had been gone for so long. Without thinking about it, he ran to Frank's house.

"Frank!"
He hollered before he reached the door. His friend opened the front door, a curious frown on his face.

"What's up?"
Frank asked as Ben reached him.

"Get changed, quick, I have something to show you."
Ben replied excitedly. Frank nodded and took off to get changed.

Ben and Frank sped down to the beach. Frank questioned his friend, but Ben couldn't find the words to explain.

"I have to show you. Come on, follow me."
Ben gabbled as they reached the water's edge.

Ben plunged in and Frank followed. Ben led the way, deeper and further until he could see the house below them. He turned to Frank and pointed down, a grin across his face. Frank shrugged. Ben frowned and pointed again but Frank shrugged again. Ben realised Frank could not see the house, so he beckoned him to follow.

Ben once again pushed the door open and swam inside, Frank close behind him. Ben could suddenly feel the change, he could breathe. He looked over his shoulder to Frank, but he couldn't see him, just a dark shadow where his best friend had been.

Ben was suddenly afraid. He spun about in the water, searching for Frank, but only the shadow Frank was there. Ben backed away from the shadow. Something bright caught his eye. He looked to his left and on a table saw a shining crystal.

There was something moving in the crystal. Ben went closer and saw it was a picture of his best friend Frank. He picked the glimmering crystal up and gazed into it. Frank was there, moving and waving, looking terrified. Ben held the crystal up. He didn't know what to do.

The crystal seemed to lose some of its shine, like when someone breathes on a mirror. Ben couldn't see Frank so clearly. Without thinking, Ben rubbed the crystal to clear it. Suddenly Frank popped out of the crystal. In surprise Ben dropped the crystal. Frank, still looking afraid, grabbed Ben's hand and dragged him through the water, up, up, up, right through the house, towards the light above.

The boys broke the surface of the sea and swam to the shore. They plodded out of the water and flopped to the beach.

"What happened?"
Asked Ben. Frank shook his head.

"I don't know. First there was just the water, then I was inside a crystal. I could see you. It was like looking through a window."

"Couldn't you see the house?"
Ben asked. Frank shook his head again.

"But that crystal looked like the one my gran had years ago. It went missing after she died."
Frank told him.

Ben knew they would never understand their adventure, but was sure he never wanted it to happen again. From that day, whenever they went diving, Ben made sure they stayed away from the undersea house, which he could always see but Frank never could.

Alfie Stoneham

# Jack The Merman

Jack the merman had been out and about swimming with his best friend Jeff, the rainbow fish. They had been gone for some time. When they arrived back at the sea palace the sea king asked to see them.

"Whilst you were gone a great tsunami brought destruction to the palace. It cracked open the magic pearl."

"Did you say the magic pearl?"
Gasped Jack. The sea king nodded.

"Yes, three shards are missing. If we don't find them and put the pearl back together our underwater kingdom cannot survive."

Jack knew the only thing he could do was search for the shards. He was the strongest and bravest of the mer-people, so it had to be him. Without the magic pearl the sharks and the sea monsters could get into the palace. But he had no idea where to begin.

"Go to the citadel. On the central pillar you will find a map. It will lead you to the shards."
The sea king told him.

"But…"
Jack began. The sea king held up his hand.

"If ever the pearl is broken, it loses three shards, just three. The pearl sends the shards to three secret places. It leaves a map on the central pillar for the strongest, bravest merman. That is you. Go, hurry, you don't have much time. The sharks and monsters already know the pearl is cracked. They will come soon."

"Come on Jeff."
Jack said as he swam towards the citadel.

The central pillar rose to the top of the kingdom. Jack could see the glow of the magic pearl inside its shining oyster far above him. He flicked his tail and sped towards it. Below the oyster on the pillar, Jack saw a map. He pointed it out to Jeff.

"That's where the first shard is."
With Jack leading, they swam from the kingdom.

The map took them to deep dark caves. They had to go into the caves to get the shard. Jack and Jeff slowly made their way into the caves. They could just make out a faint purple glow ahead. Jack knew it was the shard, so he flicked his tail harder.

An enormous squid slid out from under a rock and blocked their path. It stretched one of its tentacles towards them. Jack grabbed Jeff and just managed to flip out of its way. The squid was so big it couldn't see where they had gone. Jack dived beneath it and came out on the other side. The shard was below him in a crack in the rocks. He grabbed it. The sea churned and swirled and they were taken back to the citadel.

Jack put the shard into one of the gaps in the pearl and the next map appeared.

"Stay with the pearl Jeff. It's too dangerous for you to come."
Jack told his little friend, but Jeff wasn't going to let Jack go by himself.

"No, we do this together, like always."
Jeff said as he swam out of the citadel. Jack grinned and followed.

The second map led to the great reef. Jack spotted the purple shard easily, hiding in the pink coral. He reached for it, but a shark with huge teeth knocked him out of the way. Jack spun in the water as the shark's mouth opened wider. All of a sudden little Jeff swam into the shark's mouth.

"No!"
Screamed Jack. Then the shark coughed and out popped Jeff, he had tickled the shark's throat. The shark kept coughing, so Jack and Jeff grabbed the shard and they were once again taken back to the citadel.

With the second shard safely in its gap, Jack looked for the next map. He saw it and knew where to go. But the last shard was much further away. Jack and Jeff swam off. Many times they had to hide from sharks and sea monsters making their way towards the kingdom. They knew they didn't have a lot of time.

Deeper and deeper they went, far under the ocean. Just when Jack thought they had gone the wrong way, he saw a tiny purple light. He pointed it out to Jeff and quickly they dived towards it. The last shard was inside a very old wrecked ship. Jack squeezed through a gap in the rotting wood, Jeff close behind. It seemed safe. There were no other sea animals around and no monsters. Jack saw the shard and reached for it. He saw a flash and a long eel snaked out from behind a lump of wood. Jack flipped over and hit the eel with his tail. The eel curled and tried to bite him, but Jeff grabbed the shard and they were both taken back to the citadel.

With all the shards in their place, the pearl spread its purple glow across the kingdom, protecting the palace and everyone in it, from the sharks and sea monsters. Jack and Jeff had saved the kingdom, at least until the next storm cracked the pearl.

Billy Fiander

# Holiday Hill

Lily and Tom lived in Lynton. Near to their home was a hill called Holiday Hill. It was steep and a great place to go for a walk. It was also a very good place to practice skipping. Tom and Lily loved to skip and enjoyed competing against each other.

One evening, Tom and Lily were high up Holiday Hill. They had skipped most of the way.

"I can skip better than you."

Lily laughed to Tom.

"No you can't, watch."

Tom replied and he shoved Lily out of the way. Lily fell down.

"Ouch!"

She squealed.

"I've landed on something."

Lily scrambled up and looked down.

"Oh, it's a baby goat. Run Tom, the nanny goat will be after us if she thinks we have hurt her baby."

Lily sped off down the hill with Tom following. They were about half way down when Lily stopped.

"Don't stop!"

Yelled Tom, flying past her.

"My bracelet. It's gone. Dad gave it to me. We have to go back."

Lily cried. Tom turned and came back to Lily.

"What about the goat?"

He asked. Lily shrugged.

"I have to find my bracelet."

Tom took her hand and together they carefully and quietly walked back up the hill. The sun was beginning to set. By the time they reached the spot where Lily had fallen, it was getting dark. Tom took out his phone and switched on the torch. A thin glow gave them just enough light to search.

As he scanned the ground for the bracelet, they heard a sound. Tom lifted the torch and two bright eyes glowed in the torchlight, it was the nanny goat. Lily put out her hand.

"I'm sorry if I hurt your baby. I didn't mean to. It was an accident."
The nanny goat nodded her head. Tom and Lily thought she was going to charge at them, but then another, very small goat appeared in the darkness. It was the baby and it wasn't hurt at all. The baby goat trotted over to Tom and Lily. In the light from the torch, Lily could see her shiny bracelet, it was stuck to the goat's coat. She gently tugged the bracelet and it came free. The baby goat went back to its mother and they both trotted back into the darkness.

Lily and Tom plodded back down the hill. They couldn't wait to get home and tell their mum and dad about their little adventure.

"Sorry Lily, I won't ever push you out of the way again."
Tom said as they reached the door to their home.

Shannon Wakenell

# Time Trap

There was an icy chill in the air. As winter came nearer the warmth got further away. It was not cold enough to freeze the water yet, but it would be soon.

Jack and Jake walked through spine tingling fog. Suddenly, Jake tripped over and hit his hand on a stone, but not just any stone, a stone with a shining diamond inside. He had hurt his hand on the stone but he didn't care much because he was interested in the stone.

Jack reached out and together the boys touched the stone but nothing happened. When they touched it the third time, they found themselves somewhere else, outside a cave, a very dark cave.

Curiously, they walked into the cold, wet cave. All along the floor there were bones of animals. Jack called Jake over and said

"Look, a hole. I wonder what's down there."

"Cool!"

Squealed Jake.

"I'm gonna have a look."

"No wait…"

Jake started to say, but it was too late. As Jack leaned over the edge, the stone slipped from his hand into the hole and the boys fell with it. They landed with a thud at the bottom of a pit. It was a booby trap, made by the Miners a long time ago.

"We have to find the stone. I think it will get us out of this pit."

Jack said.

"But where are we?"

Asked Jake.

"I think…we have gone back in time. Remember the legend we learnt, about how the Miners set a time trap. These bones are the people they have caught.”

"Oh so how do we get out?"

"The stone. The legend said something about a time stone. I think we found it. Now we have to find it again."

Jack explained to his brother.

They looked around and Jake spotted the stone. It had fallen into some animal droppings. So Jack said.

"You get it. You put your hand in, you're older."

"Only by five seconds!"

Moaned Jake

They both huffed and sulked. Then Jake tripped up again and smacked his face on an old leather glove.

"I can use this!"

He shouted.

"Ok, go on then."

Replied Jack. So Jake stuck his hand in and pulled out the time stone.

"On three, we both touch it."

Jake told his brother.

"One, two, three."

They counted together and touched the stone. Whoosh! they were back on the beach. The twins found a large heavy rock and smashed the stone. As the rock touched it, the rock and the stone disappeared. The boys had destroyed the time stone, so nobody could be trapped by the Miners again.

Ashton Foden

# A Bucket Of Sand

One calm afternoon the sea was softly rippling, the bright orange sun glowed overhead and the trees swayed in a gentle breeze. On Combe Martin beach a little girl, five-year-old Lolly, played in the sand next to her dad. She was happily building a sand castle.

As her castle with its sandy turrets got bigger and bigger, Lolly had to go back and forth to the water's edge for more water. Finally, it was big enough for Lolly to hide in.

Giggling, Lolly sat within the walls of her castle. Being so little she didn't think her dad could see her, luckily he could. Lolly felt the sand under her move. It began to sink, and she went with it. Lolly screamed. Her dad saw the sand covering his daughter. He grabbed her hands and pulled her out. He tried to brush the sand off of Lolly, but it stuck to her.

Lolly's dad lifted her in his arms and carried her to the sea. Gently he poured water over her to remove the sand, but as it fell away it left her skin glittering. Lolly smiled at her dad.

"Can we swim?"
She asked. Her dad smiled back and walked into the sea with her.

"Stay close."
He told her.

Lolly started paddling about in the water. It was warm and felt very light. She put her head under the waves and saw a jelly fish swimming towards her.

"Hello."
The jelly fish spoke and Lolly could hear it. She opened her mouth and no seawater went in.

"Hello."

Lolly greeted the jelly fish back. She was surprised she could talk to the jelly fish and it could talk back.

"You found a bucket of magic sand."

The jelly fish told her.

"It made your skin shine, like scales, so anytime you're in the sea you can swim with the sea animals and talk to us."

Lolly was very happy. She swam about, staying close to her dad, but every time she put her head under the water she could talk to the jelly fish. She had so much fun she didn't want to get out, but her dad said it was getting late.

When Lolly came out of the sea she told her dad about the jelly fish. He smiled and said.

"How nice Lolly. That was quite an adventure."

Of course he thought it was just a five-year-old's imagination, especially as her skin wasn't glowing anymore.

Lolly was sad though. She thought the magic had worn off. She had her bath and washed off all the salt and sand from the beach. Her dad read her story for bed and she snuggled down and slept, dreaming of the jelly fish.

In the morning Lolly and her dad went to the beach again. Lolly didn't want to play in the sand, she wanted the water. Her dad walked her into the sea and stood close. Lolly once again splashed about and then she put her head under the water. She opened her mouth and no seawater went in.

"Jelly fish, where are you?"

She called. The jelly fish swam towards her, and with it were little fish and other sea creatures. Lolly was so excited. The magic wasn't gone. She looked at her hands and saw they were shining like scales.

Every time Lolly went into the sea she could swim, play and talk to the creatures of the water. As she grew she swam further and further, exploring the oceans and making underwater friends. Never again did she tell her dad or anyone else about her magic skin, or her undersea adventures.

Ellie Tearall

# The Finding

Akai Madovic was an ordinary guy, living in an ordinary house on an ordinary street in Combe Martin. He had an ordinary peaceful life. He worked for the council, liked his job and his way of life.

Every morning, Akai would wake up and say. "I need a coffee." He would leap out of his ordinary bed, walk down his ordinary corridor and make an ordinary cup of coffee. Then he would set off for work.

Half way through Akai's ordinary day everything changed. He spotted a poster on all the poles in the village. It was a wanted poster. There was a criminal loose in the village, and there was also a reward of one million pounds for catching the criminal. Akai was amazed, he had never seen a million pounds.

At the end of the day, Akai strolled back to his ordinary home. But his thoughts were on the poster. If he caught the escaped criminal he would be rich, and maybe then he could find a nice ordinary girlfriend to share his ordinary life with.

That evening Akai set out to try and find the criminal. He searched and searched the village, but there was no sign of the menace. Then he had an idea. Maybe the convict was hiding in the woods. Akai plodded up into the hills overlooking the village. The trees were thick with green leaves, the bushes heavy with flowers.

All night Akai searched. As the sun began to rise on another ordinary day, and Akai was ready to give up and re-join his ordinary life, he heard a noise, a rustle and crack of twigs. Carefully and quietly he sneaked up to a bush. The criminal was hiding underneath it. Akai yanked him out. The criminal was tired and Akai was strong, so he was able to hold onto him.

Akai walked the convict down and out of the woods to the ordinary police station. But there was nothing ordinary about the look of shock the police officer gave Akai though.

"Do I get my million pounds now?"
Asked Akai as he handed the criminal over.

"That and a knighthood from the Queen for catching this one. He's very dangerous."
The policeman replied. Akai jumped with joy as he left the police station.

Akai grinned all the way back to his ordinary home. He opened his ordinary door and went to his ordinary bedroom. He laid on his ordinary bed and thought about how spectacular and extraordinary it would be to get knighted by the Queen.

Matthew Ayres

# Alex And Her Strange Adventure

Alex lived in Combe Martin, and every night at midnight she would go for a stroll along the beach. It was her favourite time, when the beach was quiet and no one else was about.

One night Alex was happily skipping along the sand as usual. The moon was bright and a soft breeze lifted her long blonde hair away from her face. Waves gently lapped the beach, pebbles clicking together as the water rolled over them. Everything was normal, at first.

As Alex dipped her toes into the waves she felt a chill in the air. She frowned. She stared out to sea and saw what looked like a tsunami of mist rolling in. Alex was afraid. She backed up out of the water away from the fogginess that was rapidly closing in.

The mist reached the shore quickly. Then it stopped. Alex heard a noise, a squelching sound, and out of the mist emerged a figure. At first Alex couldn't make it out, then she froze in terror. The figure was half eel and half monster. It had dagger like teeth, sharp horns and slimy looking scales.

"Ahhh!"
Screamed Alex as she turned to run.

"Wait, don't run. I won't hurt you."
The monster called out, its voice soft and gentle. Alex stopped. She was still afraid but didn't run away.

"What's your name?"
The monster asked.

"Um…m…my name is…Alex."
She stammered.

"Well hello Alex. I might look ugly and scary but I'm nice really."

The sea monster told her.

Alex began to calm down. Even though the sea monster did look very frightening, it hadn't tried to hurt her.

"Will you be my friend?"

The sea monster asked shyly. Alex felt sorry for the sea monster.

"Yes I will."

She replied. The sea monster smiled, showing its dagger teeth.

"Would you like to come for a ride across the sea?"

It asked her. Alex nodded and walked up to the sea monster.

The sea monster bent low and Alex climbed onto its back. Alex was surprised. The monster's scales were not slimy but smooth, and the horns that stuck out of its head were a beautiful navy blue, and not sharp at all.

"Your horns are so pretty and my favourite colour."

Alex told the sea monster.

"Hold onto them tight."

It replied. Alex did and the monster dived into the sea, taking the mist with it.

Alex felt excitement inside as the sea monster swam across the waves, far out to sea. The mist was gone and the moon shone down on them brightly. In the distance Alex could see a rocky island.

"That's my home."

Called out the sea monster and swam faster. They came to the island and the sea monster slid onto the rocks and into a cave. Alex thought the cave was going to be dark and smelly but got a big surprise. Inside, the cave was bright and pretty.

"Oh it's lovely."

Exclaimed Alex. The sea monster smiled with joy.

"Would you like some tea and cake?"

It offered. Alex was again surprised, but accepted.

Alex and the sea monster chatted whilst they had their tea and cake. Alex found out the sea monster was very lonely. It told her that most creatures and humans ran away from it because it looked so frightening, and would never stop long enough to find out it wasn't. Alex thought she had nearly been one of them.

Finally, it was time to go home. Once again Alex clung to the sea monster's back and it swam her back to Combe Martin. On the beach Alex gave the sea monster a hug.

"You look scary but you're not. Your home should be dark and wet, but

it's not. I've found out tonight that I shouldn't judge on what things appear to be. I like being your friend, and anytime you want to see me, I'll be here on the beach at midnight, every night."
She said. The sea monster grinned with happiness.

Finally, it had found someone who wasn't afraid of it, a friend who would spend time with it. As it slipped back into the clear sea, it knew it would come back and see Alex very soon.

Olivia King

# Bad Boys

There were two boys who lived in Combe Martin, Mickey and Jim. They were both fifteen and often got into trouble. They would often upset the other villagers, by riding their bikes in front of cars, shouting in the street late at night and kicking sand at people on the beach.

No one seemed able to stop them from being like this. Their parents had tried, their teachers had tried, and the local police officer had too. Nothing worked. Mickey and Jim didn't care, they enjoyed doing bad things.

One night the village was woken up by a deep rumbling. It echoed all the way from seaside to the top of the village. It didn't last long, just a few seconds and when it stopped, it didn't come back.

In the morning, Mickey and Jim rode their bikes down to the beach. They were hoping it would turn out to be a nice day. That way more people would be outside, more people to annoy. But right then it was dull and the beach was deserted.

"Aw, there's no one here."
Moaned Mickey.

"Hmm, but look, the beach looks weird."
Jim replied.

The boys dropped their bikes and plodded onto the sand. The beach was strange. There were huge mounds of sand all over. They reached the first one and Mickey climbed up onto it. Jim followed. They grinned at each other. The mounds of sand would be perfect for kicking about. Mickey lifted his foot and booted the top of the mound.

"Ouch!"
He yelled. Just under the sand was a large rock. Jim brushed away the sand

uncovering the rock. It glittered and shone. Together they put their hands on the rock to pull it out. As they touched it, everything around them wobbled and they began to fall from the mound.

Mickey and Jim landed with a thud. They were no longer on the beach but in the playground of their primary school.

"What…how…?"

Squealed Jim, grabbing Mickey. Suddenly there were small children all around them playing in the playground.

"Hey watch out!"

Mickey yelled as a little boy ran towards him, being chased by two other boys, but the children went straight through him.

"Jim, what's happened? Are we dead?"

Mickey cried in terror. Jim was staring at the children.

"Look Mickey, look properly."

Jim said. Mickey looked about, then frowned.

"Oh!"

He gasped. Jim nodded.

"They're us, when we were little. We've gone back in time."

Mickey stared in shock, then put his hand over his face.

"Jim, look what we did."

The boy who was being chased was on the ground. He was crying and the other two boys were laughing at him and poking him.

"I…I remember doing that."

Jim stammered.

"And we kept on doing it didn't we? We kept on doing stuff, even now we're fifteen. We're horrible Jim, really horrible."

"We are Mickey. If we get back to our own time we should change, stop being bad."

Mickey nodded.

"Yeah Jim, I think so too. But how do we get back?"

The children in the playground disappeared. Everything became still and quiet. A rumble came from under their feet and a mound of sand lifted them up. Glittering and glowing on its top was the rock. Jim nudged Mickey and together they touched it. Everything wobbled and then they were back on the beach in their own time.

"We're back Jim, we're back."

The sun was shining and there were many villagers on the beach. When they saw Mickey and Jim they pulled their children close, expecting the boys to kick up the sand.

"We're sorry!"
Called out Jim.

"Yeah, really sorry for all the bad stuff. We're not going to be like that anymore, we promise!"
Shouted Mickey, and to prove it, they got their bikes and rode up the village, keeping out of the way of cars. They kept their promise, and soon the villagers trusted them, and Mickey and Jim realised it was much better being nice.

Callum Ford

# Little Fish

Rachel and her best friend Laylor, stood at Rachel's bedroom window looking down on the bay of Combe Martin. Rachel's house was right on the edge of the rocky cliffs, the beach far below. From her window they could see a thick fog rolling in across the sea. It looked like a dark grey blanket slowly creeping towards the beach.

"We can't go rock pooling in that."
Laylor stated.

"Oh don't be a wimp. It's only a little bit of fog, we'll just get a bit wet, that's all."
Rachel replied, turning away from the window and strolling to the door. Laylor sighed, following her friend.

The girls gathered their rock pooling gear and left the house. It was warm on the top of the cliff, the fog hadn't reached them yet.

"Come on!"
Rachel called to Laylor as she sped down the path to the bay. On the way down it began to get colder, the fog blotting out the warmth of the sun. By the time they reached the sandy beach, it was quite chilly.

"Brr, maybe we should have stayed in."
Laylor complained. Rachel laughed at her friend.

"It won't last."
She told her, as she carefully made her way along the walkway to the deepest rock pools.

Laylor followed along the slippery path until they reached their favourite pool. It looked deep and dark in the fog hanging over it. Rachel put her bucket down and dropped her crab line into the pool. Laylor did the same. For some time, the two girls sat quietly waiting for something to bite.

"It's getting warmer."

Laylor whispered after a while. Rachel looked about. A soft gentle breeze was rippling the top of the water, the path was drying and an orange glow above was scaring the fog away.

"Told you. The sun's coming out. Look, the pool is getting clearer."

Rachel pointed to the water.

The girls peered into the rock pool. They could see movement as tiny fish darted about under the water. Laylor watched as a crab grabbed her bait, but quickly it escaped into the sea weed. Rachel wiggled her line and felt a tug. She pulled it up and out of the water, but instead of a crab on the end she saw a small purple and turquoise fish.

"Oh how pretty."

She murmured.

Rachel held the fish over her bucket. As she began to lower it into the salty water she heard a squeak. Laylor stopped what she was doing and stared.

"What was that?"

She asked. Rachel leaned closer to the fish.

"Help us."

She heard the fish say in a high voice. Rachel looked at Laylor in shock.

"It spoke. The fish spoke. Did you hear it?"

Laylor nodded.

"What's wrong. How can we help?"

Laylor asked, taking charge. The pretty little fish opened its mouth and spoke again.

"There's some bottles in the rock pools, right at the bottom. They have stuff in them that is polluting the water and harming the sea creatures."

"We have to get help!"

Rachel squealed.

"I have a fish tank at home I can put you in to keep you safe. Then when the pools are cleaned up, I can put you back. Come on Laylor, we have to hurry."

The girls ran back up the path to Rachel's house. Quickly Rachel tipped the little fish into her tank and sped from her room to find her mum. She found her in the garden and hurriedly explained about the bottles. She didn't dare tell her mum about the fish, she didn't think she would believe her.

Rachel's mum called Laylor's mum, who rang some of her friends. They arranged to meet on the beach and set off straight away. The sun was shining brightly as they reached the soft sand. Soon, quite a crowd had gathered. The crowd followed Rachel and Laylor to the rock pool. The water was now clear enough to see the bottom.

"Look there."
Pointed Rachel. They could all see the bottles.

All day, more and more villagers joined the group, going from pool to pool clearing the bottles. By the time the sun was beginning to set over the bay, all of the bottles had been collected. The villagers of Combe Martin had saved their rock pools.

"How did you know?"
Rachel's mum asked as she walked back up the cliff with her and Laylor. Rachel smiled at Laylor.

"A little fish told us."
She giggled.

"Don't you mean a little bird?"
Replied her mum.

"Oh no, a little fish is right."
Said Laylor, sharing a secret smile with her friend.

Paige Chater

# Choose Your Side

The sand covered him. Gold silky sand was over his head. Seana then heard a sound, the sea. Crashing waves were coming to save him like dashing heroes. They wiped the army of gritty sand from his head, their crystal blue tips lifting him out of the pit of unforgiving death. Softly, like a life boat the sea floated Seana off the beach to safety.

The next day Seana was taken to the beach again by his mum. He didn't want to go after what had happened the day before. He tried to explain to his mum that the sand was trying to hurt him. But his mum didn't listen. She was too busy watching the people on the beach eating ice-creams, the surfers surfing, the rock-poolers rock-pooling and the sun shining. She had no time for Seana.

Seana couldn't stay on the beach, the sand was too dangerous. So when his mum wasn't looking he quietly left.

"'Ello."

A deep gravelly voice came from behind him as he walked home. Seana stopped and turned. He saw a big bulky boy. His first thought was that the boy was going to hurt him.

"Hi."

A softer voice came from behind the big lad and a small girl stepped forward.

"This is Rocks and I'm Pebbles."

Said the girl.

"Come back to the beach Seana. We won't let Sand hurt you."

Seana was shocked. He had no idea how these two knew what had happened to him. Pebbles saw the frown on his face.

"Seana, you are part of the sea. Rocks and I are part of the beach. Sand is too, and he likes to soak up the sea whenever he can. We will be your friends, help the sea protect you from Sand."

Seana thought about his mum. He had left her on the beach. With Rocks and Pebbles by his side he rushed back, but she was nowhere to be seen, just a new sand dune where he had left her. He knew he should be sad, but he wasn't. She hadn't listened to him when he tried to tell her what Sand had done to him. She had been far too interested in other things to bother about him.

Seana stood staring at the dune, Rocks and Pebbles by his side. He felt the silky, gold sand tickle his feet as it began to suck him in. Rocks and Pebbles grabbed him as Sand became a huge sandstorm swirling around them. Calm sea water rose up into a crashing storm of waves, beating Sand back away from Seana, Rocks and Pebbles. Sand had no choice but to leave them alone. He wasn't strong enough to challenge them all. Maybe it was time for him to change sides too, like Rocks and Pebbles had done.

Charley Beckett

# Playing Tricks

Heather, Kylie and Lauren were at the beach. No one else was there. It was a lovely sunny day, perfect for swimming in the warm, blue water of Combe Martin bay. As the waves lapped over their feet they felt the magic of the sea. Suddenly the day went grey and the magic was gone.

Huge waves rushed towards them, cold and dangerous.

"What's happening?"

Cried Lauren in fear.

"I don't know."

Screamed Kylie, as pebbles bashed against her under the water. Heather, the eldest, grabbed the other two and at the top of her voice yelled.

"Help, please someone help!"

As quickly as it became rough, the sea calmed and went still and quiet. The girls plodded onto the beach and flopped down in the sand.

"What was that?"

Asked Kylie. Heather began to shake her head, then stopped. A strange, deep sound was coming from the entrance to the beach.

"Come on you two, let's get off the beach and see what's making that noise."

She said to Kylie and Lauren.

The three girls crept up to the entrance to the beach, keeping low behind the wall. As they got nearer the sound got louder.

"I can't see anything."

Whispered Lauren. Heather stretched up a little and peeked over the wall. She gasped. An enormous claw was resting on the edge of the wall. She couldn't see the rest of the creature, but expected it to be huge.

"Boo!"
All three girls jumped as the deep sound became a voice.
"Got you!"
Shouted a normal human voice, and a face appeared over the wall.
The girls stood up. They were quite cross. The face belonged to a boy
they all knew, a boy who often played tricks on other people.
"You!"
Squealed Heather as the boy hopped over the wall onto the sand. In one hand
he held the claw and in the other a peculiar object.
"It's a voice changer."
He said into the object, the sound coming out deep and strange. He then burst
out laughing. The girls were still cross with him, but were relieved too.
"Come on, let's go back to our spot on the beach."
Said Kylie.
The boy followed them to where they had been enjoying the day. When
they got there Lauren stopped and looked down. In the sand she saw a huge
paw-print.
"Oh ha, ha, very funny. Well it doesn't scare us now."
She said to the boy.
"Um…I didn't do that."
He replied in a shaky, scared voice, his eyes bulging as he looked out to sea.

Holly Green

# Doughnut

Jeff the dog was on a boat. It wasn't any old boat. It belonged to Bob, Jeff's owner. Bob was sound asleep, his fishing rod dragging through the water. Jeff watched the fishing line, waiting for a bite, but nothing was happening.

Jeff closed his eyes and dozed. The boat rocked gently at first, then it began to tilt from side to side. Jeff opened his eyes. The sky was black with thick clouds and rain was falling.

Jeff nudged Bob awake just as thunder boomed overhead. Bob tried to pull his rod in but it wouldn't budge. He tugged and tugged. The rod came out of the water but a huge shark was on the end of it. The shark opened its mouth and took a bite out of the boat. Seawater flooded into the hole in the boat and it began to sink.

"Jump!"

Shouted Bob to Jeff. They both leapt over the shark into the water. Jeff swam to Bob and let him cling to his thick coat. Jeff kicked hard and swam away from the shark. The shark didn't notice, it just carried on eating the sinking boat.

With the storm dark and dangerous, swirling and churning the sea, Bob clung to his dog. Jeff battled the waves, getting more and more tired. Soon, all he could do was keep his paws moving enough so they didn't sink.

Jeff and Bob floated about in the stormy sea. Then Jeff saw a huge ring up ahead. He swam to it. It was a giant doughnut. They climbed onto the doughnut. Now they had both a boat and food. As the doughnut floated across the sea towards the beach, Jeff and Bob munched on it.

Finally, they could see the bay of Combe Martin. Luckily for them it was close enough to swim to because there wasn't much left of the doughnut.

They jumped into the water, both a lot fatter than when they set out, and paddled to the shore and safety.

Caleb MacKenzie

# Girl On The Roof

Elizabeth sat on the edge of the cliff overlooking the bay of Combe Martin. The wind brushed through her long hair and the sea sang to her from below. Seagulls flapped their wings above her and white horses galloped to the edge of the shore, disappearing into the golden sand. Then she was falling.

"Wake up. Are you ok?"
Elizabeth heard a voice. She opened her eyes and a boy was looking down at her.

"Um…what happened?"
Elizabeth asked. She felt a bit confused. The boy laughed.

"You tell me. You landed on my roof."

Elizabeth sat up and looked about. She didn't recognise the place.

"Are you ok? Look my name is Tom. What's yours?"
The boy said in a gentle voice.

"I think so. Um…I'm Elizabeth, but everyone calls me Izzy."
She replied.

"Well Izzy, how did you end up on my roof? There's nothing above us but the cliffs, and I'm sure you can't fly."

Elizabeth stared up. The straight edge of the jagged cliffs stared back, a tiny strip of green grass at the top the only colour against the grey rocks. A flash of sunlight bounced off the white feathers of a seagull, and suddenly everything came flooding back to Elizabeth.

"Oh, I know!"
She gasped. Tom took her hand.

"Tell me."
He said quietly.

Elizabeth sat forward and wrapped her arms around her knees. Tom settled next to her and waited. She took a deep breath and began.

"My house, my home is up there."
She pointed to the top of the cliffs. Tom frowned. He knew the cliffs, and knew there were no houses up there, but he stayed quiet and let her continue.

"It's cold, well it was then. Dad lit the fire to keep us warm and mum had a pot of thick stew cooking over it. The wind was howling outside and the sea was pounding the rocks. Ah, it was a storm, a big one. Thunder crashed above us and lightning flashed, over and over. Then it hit the chimney and blew the fire out across the room.

The curtains caught light and then the furniture. Soon the whole house was on fire. Dad tried to put it out but it was too big. Mum helped, but it was no good. The last thing dad did, before the fire took them both, was pick me up and throw me out of the window to save me.

But our house is, was, close to the cliff and the window he threw me from was on the cliff side. He didn't know. The smoke was so thick and the fire so hot, he couldn't see."

Elizabeth stopped talking and looked at Tom. She nodded at the same time he realised what she was saying.

"I was thrown over the edge. Your house must be new Tom."
Tom nodded back.

"It was nice talking to you Tom, but I think I have to go now."
Tom watched as Elizabeth faded before his eyes.

"Goodbye Izzy. Maybe one day I will see you again."
He felt a soft breeze ripple his hair and believed he probably would.


Daisy Pash

# Halloween Disaster

Knock, knock, knock. Al and John banged on another door. "Trick or treat." They yelled for the hundredth time, or so it seemed. The door to the old house silently swung open, but there was no one behind it and there weren't any sweets. The two boys backed away, it looked far too creepy to stay. As they reached the gate they heard a voice.

"Don't leave, I have sweets. Come in."
But they couldn't see anyone.

"Uh, nah, it's ok. We'll go trick or treating somewhere else."
Al called back, then he and John ran from the house. Behind them the door banged shut.

Al and John made their way down Combe Martin village trick or treating until they reached the beach. There they sat down and munched their sweets whilst they waited for the fireworks. They forgot all about the creepy old house and the voice as the display started.

When the fireworks finished, Al and John didn't want to go home.

"The tide's out, let's go to the cave."
John said jumping up. Al brushed the sand off his jeans and followed John along the walkway to the cave. They scrambled over the rocks and up to the dark mouth of the cave. Al was the first to go in, he didn't stay long.

"A ghost, a ghost!"
He came out screaming. John laughed.

"Yeah right. You won't scare me Al."

"You go in then, you'll see."
Al replied.

John grinned and walked bravely into the cave. He called back over his shoulder to Al.

"Told you, nothing. Come on in, don't be a scaredy cat."
Feeling a bit stupid, Al followed his friend into the cave. He was sure he had
seen something, but didn't want to appear scared to John.

The two boys went further into the dark cave. It was cold and damp and
Al was still nervous, not like John who was plodding along noisily.

"Will you kids stop waking me up!"
A voice echoed through the cave. Al froze and John let out a high scream. He
spun around and pushed past Al, screaming all the way out of the cave. Al
stumbled after him and all but fell from the cave entrance. Breathing heavily,
he picked himself up and saw his friend trembling on the walkway.

"Huh, I thought you were the tough one."
Al mumbled to John. Shaking his head John stammered back.

"Actually, I don't really like Halloween, it scares me."

"Halloween scares you? But you laughed at me for being scared of
ghosts."
Exclaimed Al. John nodded and began walking back to the beach.

"Well I reckon you could say this was a Halloween disaster."
He called back over his shoulder.

"You're right about that!"
Said the ghostly figure coming up behind them.

Sully Holloway

# Moor Meets Sea

It was barely six o'clock in the morning and Chip had decided to venture out early for once. He wasn't going anywhere in particular, just out for a walk. It was still dark and he couldn't see anything in front of him but a blurry mist.

As he plodded across fields the darkness began to change. At first he could make out clouds above, and gradually plants below his feet. The sun began to rise and Chip realised he was out on the moors.

In the dim light, far ahead in the distance, Chip could just make out a figure. It looked dark and brown, almost a shadow. He stopped and waited, watching as the figure came towards him. He shuddered, he had heard many stories and myths about the ghosts that haunted the moors, and was afraid this might be one of them.

The figure was still approaching. Even as the sun rose higher and the moorland grasses became greener, the figure still seemed dark and shadowy. As it got closer Chip heard a sound, a faint cough, then another. Chip let out his breath and sighed. The figure was his friend Rosy, he recognised the sound of her cough.

"What are you doing out so early?"
Rosy asked as she reached him.

"Going for a walk, for once."
Chip replied. Rosy laughed. Chip never got up early, and he never went walking on the moors, even in the middle of the day.

"Well I'm glad. It's good to see you out. You spend far too much time indoors. I come out every morning. It helps my chest, helps my cough."
Rosy told him. Chip sighed again. Rosy, his best friend had a problem with her chest. Sometimes she couldn't breathe very well.

"Well maybe I should come out every day with you. Why don't you show me the moors, you must know them very well?"

"Come on then."

Rosy said taking his hand.

Rosy led Chip across the fresh moorland. As they walked a thick mist rolled in. They couldn't see anything in front of them.

"I can smell the sea."

Chip stated and stopped.

"What is it? What's wrong?"

Rosy asked worriedly. Chip held Rosy's hand tight, pulling her close to his side.

"Don't move."

He shrieked.

All around them the mist swirled, blotting out the sunlight. They couldn't see anything, but they could hear the sound of the sea. Chip carefully moved one foot forward, sliding it along the ground until his toes felt nothing but air.

"I think we are on the edge of a cliff."

He explained. A light breeze lifted some of the fog, clearing it a little, enough for them to see rocks jutting out far below and crashing waves.

"Rosy, step back very slowly."

Chip instructed. Rosy did as he suggested and Chip followed. A few more steps and they were clear of the cliff.

"Wow, my first early morning walk turned out to be quite an adventure."

Chip gasped. Rosy laughed as she sat down on the grass.

"But look at that view."

She pointed. The sun had broken through and the mist was gone. From high up on the cliff they could see where Exmoor met the bright blue glistening sea.

Ellen Barrow

# The Cave

Adam and Jake are both twelve years old and have thick flame red hair. Most people think they are twins, but they're not. What they do share is their special powers of the sea.

Most of the time the boys are just like any other lads doing the same things other boys enjoy. They especially like to go down to Combe Martin beach and rock climb.

One sunny, warm day Adam and Jack trekked off to the beach. They strolled along the walkway chatting about their plan to climb the cliffs. As they reached the foot of the jagged rocks Jake stopped. He grinned at Adam.

"I dare you to go into the haunted cave."
Adam shrugged. He didn't want to go into the cave really, but he didn't want to let Jake know that.

"Come on then."
Adam replied and led the way to the cave entrance.

As they got closer and the dark mouth of the cave opened wider, Adam shuddered. The only time he had been into the cave was six years before, and it had frightened him nearly to death. He had heard pounding sounds and whispers, the legendary ghosts of the miners.

Taking a deep breath, Adam led the two boys into the cave. Jake nudged him from behind, prodding him to go further. Nervously, Adam slowly walked deeper into the cold, dark tunnel.

The boys seemed to walk for a long time. It was very dark, the tiny speck of light from the cave entrance way behind them. The walls were hard rock, and somewhere above them water dripped, echoing and splashing against the floor.

It seemed to Adam that the cave would never end. He was trembling and wanted to turn back, but he knew Jake was behind him and would only laugh. He took a deep breath and put one foot in front of the other. At the same time, he heard a deep laugh in the tunnel ahead. He stopped suddenly, Jake bumping into him.

"Did you hear that?"
Adam whispered. Jake put his hand on his friend's shoulder.

"Don't worry. Remember our powers Adam. Nothing, even ghosts, can hurt us."
Adam wasn't so sure, but encouraged by Jake began to move forward.

"I've got you where I want you now!"
A deep voice boomed. It was coming from all around them. The two boys heard a loud cracking sound. Rocks and boulders began to fall from above as the cave collapsed around them.

"Adam we're trapped!"
Hollered Jake. Adam felt no more fear of the ghost as he took a breath and lifted his arms. His power flowed, he could become water, filling the cave with cool fresh seawater. Jake grinned at his friend and let his own power out. He became a mako shark.

"You can't keep us trapped now."
Adam shouted to the ghostly voice, forcing his way through the rocks and parting them. Jake used his big shark body to roll the boulders out of the way, and together water and fish flowed smoothly from the cave.

Adam and Jake turned back into their human form, and like any other boys, strolled back along the walkway to the beach. Just another adventurous day for the two boys with flaming red hair and special sea powers.

Thanadol Ford

# Hide And Seek

Alice was at home alone. Her mum was out and she was waiting for her friends to come around. They were late. She'd had a text from them telling her they wouldn't be too long and she was busy texting back. Bang! Alice jumped. Bang! Then pounding on her front door. Alice knew who it was, her friends, Bella and Mackensie. They had as usual tricked her and got here sooner than they said.

Alice opened the door.

"Come on, we've got a plan."
Mackensie announced without coming in.

"What do you mean?"
Alice asked suspiciously. Mackensie and Bella always had something sneaky planned.

"Get your bike we're going to the park."
Bella explained.

Alice wasn't supposed to go out when her mum wasn't there. She had told her mum the girls were coming around and they would be listening to music. But Bella and Mackensie had other ideas.

"My mum thinks we're staying in."
Said Alice.

"So, we'll be back before she gets home."
Bella coaxed. Alice didn't want her friends to think she was a baby, so she got her helmet and bike and followed them to the park.

It was getting dark when they got to the park. Bella and Mackensie jumped off their bikes and ran to the swings. Alice nervously climbed off her bike and lowered it to the ground. She didn't like the park at night. It was too quiet and lonely, far from any houses and there were too many bushes where someone could hide.

"Hey Alice. Let's play hide and seek!"
Shrieked Mackensie.

"Um…ok. You two hide, I'll seek."
Alice replied. She didn't want to go into the darkest corners of the park and thought it would be better to be the seeker.

Bella and Mackensie ran off to hide and Bella stood with her eyes shut.

"One, two, three…"
She called out. She carried on counting out loud as everything around her went silent.

"Ninety-nine, one hundred. Coming!"
Alice yelled and opened her eyes. Feeling afraid, Alice took a few steps towards the bushes. She couldn't see Bella or Mackensie and she couldn't hear them. Bella nearly always giggled, but not tonight. Alice thought they might have tricked her and gone home, but their bikes were still where they had dropped them.

"B…Bells...Mack, wh…where are you?"
Alice called, her voice wobbling. There was no reply.

Alice spun around as she heard a rustling in one of the bushes. Then another from behind her. Before she could scream, something was put over her head and someone lifted her off her feet. Alice struggled but the person was too big. Then she was being dropped onto something flat and hard. She heard a door slam and an engine start, she was being kidnapped.

Alice managed to sit up in the now moving vehicle. Her hands and feet were tied, but she did manage to grab the thing over her head and pull it off. She was in a van and next to her was Bella and Mackensie. They were tied up too.

"What happened?"
Whispered Alice.

"We were hiding in different places and someone grabbed us and shoved us in this van. Then they went back and got you."
Mackensie told her.

"Oh, no one knows where we went."
Moaned Alice.

"Shut up back there!"
A harsh voice boomed from the front of the van. The girls went quiet, they

were too frightened to speak again. After what seemed ages the van stopped. The doors opened and a huge man pulled them out one by one. He shoved the hoods back over their heads, carried them into a house and locked them in an empty room.

Alice's mum came home at ten o'clock. She walked in with a smile, that turned to a frown, when she saw her daughter wasn't there. She checked the whole house and began to worry. She tried ringing Alice, but it kept going to voice mail. Quickly she called Bella's and Mackensie's homes and found they were missing too. They all thought the girls were at Alice's house and their phones were off too. She then called the police.

After many questions to all the parents, the police set up a search party. It didn't take them long to discover the bikes and helmets at the park. But it didn't give them any clues to where the girls were. Alice's mum, Bella's parents and Mackensie's parents were out of their minds. It seemed certain that someone had taken their children.

Hours later as the sun began to rise on another day, the police, villagers and the girls' parents searched. Alice's mum clutched her phone to her chest and nearly jumped out of her skin when it rang.

"Help us, please…"
She heard her daughter whisper before the phone cut off. Alice's mum ran to a police officer and told him about the call. It meant Alice had her phone with her and it was switched on. The police were able to locate Alice's phone and soon a team of officers were breaking down the door to the kidnapper's house.

At the hospital, the girls were checked, found to be unhurt, and then told their parents could take them home. Before they left, the families gathered together and the girls apologised.

"Never again mum. I promise I won't go out without you knowing where I am ever again."
Said Alice.

"And we won't make any sneaky plans ever again."
Exclaimed Bella, Mackensie nodding in agreement.

"We hope."
Muttered all the parents under their breath.


Layla Bacon

# The Promise

One cold mid-winter's day, a storm raged over Combe Martin. The leaves of the trees were tossed to the ground and waves bubbled wildly onto the shore. Rocks, high on the cliffs, rumbled and tumbled, crashing into the sea.

At the end of the storm, two very naughty boys, John and Bob, went down seaside to the shop. Sneakily, as they had done many times, they stole sweets from the shop and ran to the beach to eat them. The storm had torn up the beach and washed a lot of the sand away.

John and Bob strolled along the shore munching the stolen sweets, John happily kicking at the sand. His foot caught on something hard. He stopped and looked down, it was a bone. He pointed it out to Bob. The bone looked very old and they thought it was human.

"There's something inside it."
John told Bob. Bob turned it over and looked. A beautiful diamond shone and gleamed. Whilst Bob held the bone, John tried to pull the diamond out. As he touched it they heard a noise, whoosh.

The boys felt themselves falling. They closed their eyes until they thudded onto soft sand. John opened his eyes first.

"Where are we?"
Bob slowly opened his eyes.

"Oh I don't know, but I don't like it. This is not our beach and it's not winter."
He replied.

"There's a cottage over there."
John pointed.

The two boys crept closer to the cottage, right up to its walls. They peeked around a corner and saw a door. The door opened and two men stepped out.

"Did you hear that Bob?"

"No John. What was it?"

"No idea, thought it was someone out here."

John looked at Bob, his mouth hanging open in surprise. He nudged Bob to back up away from the cottage, then he whispered.

"They've got the same names as us, and they look like us, but they're old."

"Are they us in the future do you think…?"

Bob didn't finish his sentence as a strong arm came around his waist.

"Oi, who are you and what are you doing here?"

Boomed a deep voice. The other man grabbed John.

"We…we…we're you. I mean, you're us."

Stammered Bob.

The man let him go and stood back. The other man did the same.

"You can't be."

Said the older Bob. The older John leaned down and stared at the boys.

"Bob, they're right. They are us. How did you get here?"

Twelve-year-old John shrugged.

"We found a bone with a diamond in it. When we touched it we fell and landed here."

Older Bob nodded his head. He looked at older John and sighed.

"I remember that, don't you?"

Older John nodded his head too.

"But we've been here since, growing old. How did they, us get here?"

The two Bobs and the two Johns all shrugged.

"Where's the bone?"

Young John asked. As he did the older Bob and older John began to fade.

"I know what's happening!"

Shouted older Bob.

"Find the bone. But you must not take the diamond. Promise it you won't steal it or steal anything ever again. Promise."

Bob's voice faded too and with a tiny pop he and older John vanished.

Young Bob and young John ran down to the sea. They searched and searched for the bone. Finally, they found it in between two rocks. They picked it up and held it together.

"We promise not to steal the diamond. We promise never to steal anything ever again."
With a loud whoosh they began to fall. They closed their eyes, and when they landed, opened them to find they were back on their own beach, in their own time. The bone was gone and so were the sweets.

"Let's go home Bob."
Mumbled John. Bob nodded.

"No more stealing, ever."
Replied Bob, and they kept their promise.

Stanley Jenkins

# Botty's Birthday

On the morning of Botty's tenth birthday she came bouncing down the stairs ready to open her presents. There was one special one from her gran that she was more excited about opening. Wrapped in pretty paper, the present was tiny. Botty pulled off the wrapping and found a small silver box. Inside was a beautiful shiny shell threaded to a thin leather string. Botty lifted the tiny object to her ear. She heard the soft splash of water.

"Can we go to the beach, have a picnic and play in the sea?"
She begged her parents. They smiled and agreed. On the way, they picked gran up and the family happily strolled down to the beach.

It was a warm sunny day. The sand was soft and the sea a glistening blue. The beach was already busy, but Botty and her family found a nice spot and settled down. Botty began playing in the sand. She made sand castles and ate the picnic her mum had packed.

Botty began to get too hot in the sand and asked if she could go in the water. Her parents agreed. Gran said.

"I'll come with you. Is your shell safe?"
Botty nodded and held out her arm. She had tied the shell to her wrist.

When they reached the water, Botty's gran stepped straight into the sea.

"Come in Botty, it's lovely and warm."
Botty put her foot out to test the water. As soon as her skin touched the salty sea, she couldn't see clearly. Everything was blurry.

"Gran!" she called in panic. "My eyes, I can't see properly."

"It's all right Botty."
Her gran said from close by.

"You have the golden sight. Come right into the water, you'll see."

Botty stepped forward and felt the warm water covering her. Straight away she could see clearly.

"Put your head under."

Her gran said from by her side. Botty did and found she could see everything under the water clearly.

"Come with me Botty. Right under the water."

Her gran murmured taking her hand.

Botty let her gran lead her into the sea and under the waves. In surprise, she found she could breathe as well, and they could talk.

"This is amazing gran. But how?"

Botty asked as she took in all the beautiful sights under the sea.

"The shell, it's magic from deep within the ocean. With it you can be a part of the sea. I have one too, from my grandmother, she gave it to me on my tenth birthday."

Botty and her gran swam about under the sea. They played and chatted to the sea creatures and had a wonderful time. Finally, it was time to go back, and as Botty put her feet onto the warm dry sand, her sight cleared. She looked at her gran and just caught her eyes changing from gold back to blue.

Botty's parents were snoozing on the beach. They had no idea that Botty and her gran had been on an underwater adventure. Botty and her gran didn't tell them, it was their special secret.

Taya Boudier

# The Big Break

Newberry beach is great for parkouring. The river is perfect for jumping over, the rocks big enough to climb and the sea wonderful for splashing in and out of. It's also usually deserted, just right for two pro-parkourists.

Jayden and Ethan ran around risking their lives for what they loved best, parkouring. Every morning they got up and ran to Newberry beach to practice their skills. They had grown up near the beach and knew it so well it was like a second home to them.

Two minutes, just two minutes was all it took to change their lives, as one morning an unfortunate incident occurred. Running along the stones in the river, Jayden spotted a rock sticking out of the water. He made a quick turn in direction, but Ethan didn't see the rock. Ethan tripped on the rock and crashed into Jayden. They both hit the ground hard.

The pebbles beneath them gave way and a gaping hole opened up. They both fell in, landing many feet below the beach. Jayden's ankle was sprained and Ethan looked like he had a broken wrist. Their parkouring abilities could not help them there.

Above they could hear the sound of the sea. They knew the tide was coming in fast. Soon the hole would fill up with sea water and there was no way out. The first waves splashed down onto them. Cold salty water began to pool around their feet. Time was not on their side.

Another minute went by and more waves rolled over the edge of the hole. The boys were now waist deep in sea water. The walls of the hole were jagged, but went straight up. There was only one thing they could do, wait.

The water deepened, and as it rose, Jayden and Ethan clung to each other. Ethan kicked with his feet and Jayden paddled with his arms, and together they kept afloat. With seconds ticking by, the two boys reached the top of the hole with the sea water, and battled through the crashing waves until they could crawl to dry land.

Supporting each other, Jayden and Ethan made their way home. It was sometime before either of them were healed enough for parkouring again. But what they realised, was that even though parkouring was what they loved best, it was their swimming skills that had saved them.

Roman Kane

# The Field

It had been raining forever, or so it seemed to Mark and Tom. All around them the only sounds were the rushing of the river and the moaning of the wind. All around them was mist, nothing but mist.

Mark and Tom lived on a farm near Combe Martin and their job was to look after the animals, especially the sheep. As it had been raining for so long the sheep had to be kept in the barn as the fields were like swamps. This was hard for the sheep as they preferred to graze on the grass.

One morning in the pouring rain, Mark rushed from the barn and didn't close the gate properly. He didn't know he had done this until much later when Tom ran up to him.

"Mark the sheep are out!"

Yelled Tom. They dashed off to the fields and watched in horror as the sheep disappeared one by one into the soggy ground. Within seconds the sheep were all gone.

Tom and Mark ran into the field. Suddenly they were sinking too. Down, down they fell until they landed in a different world. All around them were green fields and sunshine, but there was no sign of the sheep.

"They could be anywhere."

Exclaimed Tom.

A shiny bright bird flew past them. They chased after it and it led them to the sheep.

"Well they all look ok."

Said Mark, as he watched the sheep grazing happily on the fresh grass.

"But how do we get them back to our own world?"

He added. They both looked about. There was no way out of this world. It seemed they could fall in but not fall out.

A tiny bug landed on Mark's hand. He went to brush it off but to his surprise it spoke.

"I can take you and your sheep back out."
It squeaked. Tom laughed.

"How? You're so tiny."
The bug spread its wings.

"Touch my back."
It instructed. Tom looked at Mark and shrugged. Then they each held out a finger and touched the bug. Miraculously, the bug lifted them from their feet, the sheep too and flew upwards. Up and up they all went, when all of a sudden everything changed. The sky became dark and misty and wet. Tom, Mark and the sheep all landed outside the barn, they were home. Quickly, Tom and Mark herded the sheep into the barn and closed the gate, making sure it was properly shut.

"I want to see that field."
Said Tom. Together they plodded through the mud to the field.

"See, it looks weird Mark."
Tom pointed. Mark peered at the field. They could see the water on top of the field and grass under the water. They could also just make out a dark patch.

"I bet that's where the sheep and us fell in."
Gasped Mark.

"You know Tom, sheep have gone missing from this field before, and all the time we thought it was rustlers. But I've realised it only happens when it's been raining for a long time."

"Maybe we should let them out then when it's wet. That way the sheep can get fresh grass and we know how to get them back."
Tom replied with a grin.

Zak Norman

# Woods To Sea

Max and Luke are two young boys who live in Combe Martin. They are very good friends, and spend most of their free time playing together. Sometimes, they play on the beach and in the sea, other times they explore the woods and hills overlooking the valley.

One evening, the boys were out in the woods. It was still early and still light. They had plenty of time to climb the trees and hide in the bushes before they had to be home. Luke scrambled up a tall tree pretending to be a sailor climbing the rigging. Max stayed at the bottom.

"What can you see?"
He called out.

"Nothing captain. The sea's all calm."
Luke replied. Playing at sailors was one of their favourite games.

As Luke clambered back down the tree, a few drops of rain splattered on his head. By the time he reached Max the sky had turned black with thick clouds overhead.

The two boys ran under a heavy bush as the clouds burst and rain lashed down. They had some shelter but were still getting soaking wet.

"Let's make a run for it."
Max said. Luke nodded and the two boys ducked out from beneath the cover of the bush. Just at that moment a bright flash blinded them. Terrified they ran back underneath the bush. From between the branches they could just make out a large patch of scorched earth and a broken tree trunk.

"Aliens, it's aliens."
Screamed Luke and he took off running as fast as he could, Max following close behind.

The boys crashed down the pathway, sliding and slipping on the wet mud. At the bottom where the path met the road, they stopped and looked up into the woods. They could still see flashing bright light.

"They're still coming."
Squealed Max. This time he took the lead and they sped off down the road towards the beach.

The rain was coming in torrents as Max and Luke jumped onto the sand, but at least there wasn't anything following them. Both out of breath, they plonked down on the wet beach. The sea was churning in front of them. Huge waves crashing onto the sand. Still, the boys felt safer here than in the woods.

Wet but relieved, Max and Luke watched the sea. As one enormous wave broke across the sand they heard a strange noise. They leapt to their feet just as a long tentacle appeared out of the wave, then another and another. Max and Luke backed away as a kraken broke the surface of the water, its snaky tentacles reaching for the two boys.

Screaming, the boys ran from the beach. A flash in the sky and a howling noise made them stop and look back. The kraken was slipping back under the water.

"Shall we go home?"
Luke asked. Max nodded. The rain was still pouring down and thunder rumbled overhead as they splashed through the puddles towards their homes. They reached Max's house first. Max's mum saw them coming and opened the door.

"You're soaked. Hurry in I'll get towels and call Luke's mum. Where have you been?"

"In the woods first, an alien chased us, then we ran to the beach and a kraken nearly got us."
Gabbled Max. His mum went to get towels, a smile on her face. She loved listening to their stories.

Liam Metherell

# Rocky Trap

One early morning in Combe Martin after a huge storm, two children, John and Samantha, set out across the cliffs. When they reached the edge of the rocky cliffs they stopped and looked down. The soft bubbling sea was below them and a gentle breeze around them. They were full of laughter now the storm had passed.

Just below, where the jagged rocks jutted out, John saw a beautiful diamond necklace, washed up by the storm. He gave it to Samantha and she put it on. Then they were tumbling down, down into a rocky gap. They were trapped. The necklace snagged on a sharp boulder and fell from Samantha's neck. It slipped into a crack in the boulder, but it seemed to fit the crack perfectly.

John and Samantha heard a strange rumbling sound. All around them the rocks and pebbles began to move and change shape. John and Samantha stood in their rocky trap, frozen as the rocks became people.

"You have brought us the stolen necklace."
Boomed a voice from one of the rock people.

"You have lifted the curse. We are people again."
Said another. He parted the rock with the crack in it and lifted the necklace out. He handed it to Samantha.

"Here, take it as a reward."

Samantha smiled happily and put the necklace back around her neck. Immediately she rose from the trap. John held out his hand and she took it. He rose out of the trap too, up and back to the top of the cliffs.

"Wow, that was…was strange."
John said as they landed. Samantha nodded and touched the necklace around

her throat. She felt nervous, sure something was wrong. She leaned over the edge of the cliff and gasped at what she saw. The rock people didn't look like people anymore. Instead they looked like huge grey lumps of stone with evil faces.

"Oh no. Look John, look what we have done!"
Shrieked Samantha. John looked down.

"Run Samantha, they're coming."

As the two children tore across the cliffs, they heard the crashing of the rock people climbing up. John and Samantha fled along the path, down onto the beach. They ran onto the sand right to the water's edge. They had nowhere left to go.

"Take the key, unlock the door inside the cave. Put the necklace in the room. Hide it, you will see how."
A beautiful voice rang out from above. John gazed up and opened his mouth in wonder. Samantha followed John's gaze. She too got a surprise. Silver keys were falling like rain. They landed on the sand around them.

"Which one!"
Hollered John.

"Choose."
Replied the voice.

A loud thundering rumble came from behind them. Samantha grabbed John's arm in panic. The rock people had found them. John reached down and snatched a key from the sand. It turned to gold in his hand.

"This must be it. Come on hurry!"
John yelled above the sound of the crashing rocks.

John raced along the walkway, Samantha close behind. They reached the cave and dived inside. At first it was too dark to see, but the golden key lit the way. They went deeper into the cave, the sound of the rock people nearby. The key glowed more brightly and in its light they saw the door.

John pushed the key into the lock and turned it. They heard a click and the door swung open. Inside they saw a small room. It was filled with necklaces, just like the one Samantha was wearing. Now they knew how to hide it. Samantha dragged the necklace from her throat and buried it deep in the pile. She pushed the other necklaces around. It was impossible to tell which necklace was which.

John and Samantha left the room and locked it back up. As John pulled the key from the lock it turned to a golden mist, and as it spread down through the cave, it disappeared.

Everything was suddenly quiet. John and Samantha slowly and nervously walked back to the cave entrance. There were no rock people waiting for them. But there were far more big rocks and boulders at the foot of the cliffs than there had been before. Samantha sighed.

"If we ever find any jewellery again, I'll leave it where we find it." John nodded in agreement as he took Samantha's hand and strolled back along the walkway.

Mellissa Bacon

# The Wonders Of Combe Martin

Once there were two boys, best friends, same age, but they lived in two very different places. So different, anyone would think they were on different planets. One boy named Jack, lived in the village of Combe Martin, a place in the countryside by the sea and full of nature. The other boy Alex, lived in the big city of New York, a place that never slept and noise always boomed through the air.

One summer, Alex came to visit Combe Martin to see Jack. They didn't see each other very often, sometimes just once a year and always in New York. So this time, Jack was eager to show his friend the wonders of the village of Combe Martin.

When Alex saw the high street of Combe Martin, he felt a laugh tickle the back of his throat. When he met up with Jack, he began to boast about New York.

"There are so many shops in my city and so much more to do. Far more than here."

Jack disagreed with him.

"You rely too much on your manmade structures. Here, we like the secrets that nature gives us. In New York you barely have a sight of anything natural."

After the argument Jack decided to show his friend the woods around Combe Martin. He was sure they would change Alex's mind. The boys explored the woody hills. They watched the trees wave their branches like friendly hands and saw the emerald leaves tremble in the breeze. But in the end, it wasn't enough to convince Alex.

Alex just stood in misery and moaned. He didn't even look at Jack who could see his friend was not at all impressed. Jack worried that it was hopeless. He had shown Alex everything, the swaying flowers bright with colour, the rushing stream, the soft blades of green grass and the twisty vines hanging from the trees. But the more he showed, the less interested Alex became.

Jack leaned against a tree in deep concentration. What else could he show his friend.

"Of course."
He muttered to himself.

"The beach. Why didn't I think about it before?"
Combe Martin beach was amazing in summer and if that couldn't convince his friend nothing could.

"Come on Alex, one more thing to show you."

Jack darted off towards the seaside, Alex stomping miserably behind. Jack led them to the top of the carpark. When he got there he stopped and waited for Alex to catch up.

"There!"
Jack called out, pointing to the beach below. Alex looked down and his eyes froze on the sight of the beach. He couldn't look away. The golden sand glowed, a strip of beauty kissed by the berry blue sea gently lapping at its edge. On the horizon, a herd of white horses were galloping towards the beach that looked like melting butter. Alex was stunned. He had never seen anything like it.

Alex grabbed Jack and the two boys ran towards the seaside. When they reached the beach they slowed, strolling along the rocky walkway to the rock pools. Alex knelt down and stared at the sea-life in the giant fish bowls, sometimes catching sight of a jellyfish. He stretched out his fingers and touched the water. It felt soft and warm against his rough skin. He put his whole hand into the pool, sliding it down near to the bottom. The water soothed him and he felt more relaxed than he had ever felt. He glanced back over his shoulder and saw behind him a perfect view of Combe Martin. In that moment he realised, the village he had laughed at was actually full of amazing wonders.


Charlie Wyborn

ABOUT THE AUTHORS

The authors of this book are all children from Combe Martin Primary School in North Devon, United Kingdom, in years four, five and six. The project was the idea of author Stephanie M Turner, who spent time in the school with the children, instructing and encouraging them on how to develop their ideas. The results are the wonderful stories the children created.